# UNBROKEN

## ANNE SCHRAFF

SADDLEBACK
EDUCATIONAL PUBLISHING
www.sdlback.com

ISBN-13: 978-1-61651-960-5
ISBN-10: 1-61651-960-6
eBook: 978-1-61247-647-6

Printed in Guangzhou, China
NOR/0413/CA21300570

17 16 15 14 13    2 3 4 5 6

# CHAPTER ONE

The day was sunny, but a cold wind was blowing. It had rained on Tuesday, and a sprinkling of snow lay on the distant mountains. David Morales wore just a sweater, and he wished he had a warmer jacket. He stood with the deputy sheriff looking down the road. He expected to see a pickup truck appear anytime.

David had been living for this day for two years, and many times he thought the day would never come. But now he was terribly nervous. His stomach hurt. He felt as though he could still hear the chains that he'd worn on his wrists and legs two years ago. He could hear them even in his sleep. He felt as though he'd spent years on an alien planet. Now that he had returned to Earth, he felt like the alien. He wasn't sure what to say, how to act.

He was almost afraid to leave prison life.

"There it is," the sheriff nodded. He was a pleasant fellow, nicer than most of the officers at the prison. They all did their jobs with reasonable manners. They were dealing with convicts, not hotel guests. Some of the inmates had done lesser crimes than David's, but many had done much worse. The men who ran the prison had to be tough.

"So, you got everything?" the sheriff asked David, looking at his small duffel bag.

"Yes, thank you, sir," David replied numbly. He stared as the pickup grew closer. The deputy shook hands with David. Then he said what he said to them all as they leave. "Good luck to you, man. I hope I never see you again."

David managed a thin smile and responded, "You won't."

Paul Morales brought the pickup to a stop and jumped out. He grabbed his brother in a bear hug, and the brothers embraced for a long time. Then Paul tossed the duffel bag into the truck. He nodded toward the deputy, who turned and headed back into the gate. Paul and David climbed into the cab, David on the passenger side.

David's legs felt rubbery. He almost fell while getting in the cab. He pulled the door shut.

"Seat belt, dude," Paul reminded him.

"Oh yeah," David said, clicking it around his waist.

"Yeehah!" Paul screamed as they drove away from the prison. David looked at his kid brother and thought he hadn't changed. Then Paul made a suggestion. "Wanna get somethin' to eat? There's a diner down the road. Pancakes, sausages, nice hot coffee."

"I don't know if I could keep it down," David responded.

Paul looked over and briefly clapped a hand on his brother's shoulder. "You'll do fine," he assured him. "You're thin, *hermano*. You and me, we're the same height, and I think I got fifteen pounds on you at least. We gotta do something about that."

David stared at the hills and mountains in the distance. He'd looked at them during all the days, the weeks, the months, and the years he was in prison. But they looked different now that he was free. They looked completely different, though he didn't know exactly how. As they drove, David vaguely remembered the landmarks. But the grocery store he used to go to was closed and boarded up. There were no more gas stations on the corner where he remembered two.

They pulled into the diner lot, parked, and walked in. They sat down in a booth in the back. Paul ordered two big breakfasts of pancakes, sausage, bacon, with lots of syrup and butter.

"You look like the deer in the headlights, dude," Paul remarked.

"Yeah," David responded. "I feel like that." He looked at the puffy light brown pancakes. He opened the syrup containers and watched the golden river run over the melting pats of butter. He realized he was hungry. He had never been so hungry in his adult life. He wolfed down the pancakes, the fat little brown sausages, and the crispy bacon. He had to keep wiping his chin with a napkin.

Paul laughed. "Dude, you gotta brush up on your table manners. We're eating with a real nice family on Sunday."

"What?" David gasped. "Who—what are you talking about?"

"Ernesto Sandoval and his family," Paul replied. "Remember me tellin' you about him when I came to visit you?"

"Oh yeah, your friend," David recalled, pitching another forkful of pancakes into his mouth. "His father teaches at Chavez. But why would he . . . why would *they*, I mean . . .?" David wiped his chin again.

"That's who he is, David," Paul explained. "There's not a more decent human bein' on this planet than Ernie. On top of

5

that, he's a fun guy. He has this other friend, Abel Ruiz, a great guy too. Those two are my best homies, man. Abel's gonna cook *carne asada* for us. Let me tell you, the kid is still only a senior in Chavez, but he's a genius in the kitchen. My chick Carmen is comin' too. You met her."

"Paul, won't that be like . . . awkward?" David asked. "I've spent the last two years talking to cons. What am I gonna say? What if they ask me what prison was like? Man, I'll freak."

"Don't worry, David," Paul assured him. "It'll be cool. Ernie has these two little sisters—little *muchachas*—cutest little trolls you ever saw. They'll be there too."

"Two little girls?" David groaned. "I'll probably scare the heck outta them! An ex-convict! They'll hide under the table and cry!"

Paul laughed. "Dude, would I get you into a bad situation?" Paul leaned forward as he spoke with his brother. "Listen up, *hermano*. You're all I got in the way of blood, and I'm all you got. I got your back, David. Don't you ever forget that. Remember when we were kids and sometimes we wound up in the same foster home? Didn't I always have your back, even though I was younger? I'm a tough *hombre*, David. I'm not gonna let anything bad happen to you."

They finished their breakfast and headed for Paul's apartment on Cardinal Street. As they got closer to Paul's place, David spoke. "I hope you didn't go to much bother getting ready for me. Just a curtain'd be a fine room divider. I'll be fine on a sleepin' bag. Believe me, after sleepin' on that hard cot in prison, a sleeping bag's gonna feel like a real mattress."

"Nah, no problem, dude," Paul replied, grinning.

"What're you grinning about, man?" David asked.

"Nothing," Paul responded, pulling into the apartment parking lot. "I got a bigger apartment now. Not the little one we used to have."

The two young men went up the three steps that led into the downstairs apartment. David's eyes widened as he stepped inside. "Nice, man . . . hey, a bookcase for a room divider . . . lookin' good," he marveled.

"Room on the left is yours, David," Paul nodded. "Just stash your duffel bag. I bought some stuff for you to wear, nothin' much—tees and jeans, socks and shorts. They're in the chest of drawers. Got that shampoo you used to like, the shavin' cream, and other stuff."

"Paul," David gasped, "the bed! It looks so nice . . . like new or something! And the chest of drawers! You didn't go and spend your hard–earned dough—"

"It was all free, man," Paul explained, still grinning. "You know my chick, Carmen? Well, her sister's married to a rich dude named Ivan Redondo. I think you know him. Didn't Ivan teach your Bible class in prison? He's one of our homies now. His folks are rollin' in dough, and he just borrowed some furniture they never use. He's high on you, man. He's kinda geeky, but he's my friend now."

They stood in silence for a moment. David was overwhelmed. Paul remarked, "Me and my homies fixed up the place. Nice job, eh?"

"*Muy bien, mi hermano. Muy bien,*" was all David could murmur.

David sat down on the chair next to the bed. He put his hand to his face and covered his eyes. "Bro, I . . . don't deserve any of this. I screwed up so bad. You were just a kid, finishin' high school. You were workin' like a dog at the burger stand and staying out of trouble. I was your big brother. I shoulda been lookin' out for you, but then me and my lousy homies started boosting laptops and cell phones. I wanted stuff I couldn't afford. I was a selfish creep, hanging out with scum and dating no-good chicks who just wanted jewelry to hang around their necks and stick in their ears."

David's voice was filled with regret and sorrow. He sighed deeply and continued speaking.

"I didn't care about you. I didn't care that you had to come to my trial and sit there. You hadda watch your rotten brother convicted and sent to prison. I didn't care how much that ripped your gut, Paul. I don't deserve any of this. You could just slip me a twenty and tell me to get lost and make my own way. That'd be only fair. That'd be just what I deserve."

"That's all true, dude," Paul agreed. "But what's done is done. And I love you, man. You're my brother. 'S long as we're on the subject, I want you to lissen up now. *Hermano*, you screw up again, and you'll think you died and went to hell. I swear that. I'm gonna be so on you. You'll probably have fond memories of the worst day you ever spent in prison. In the meantime, get outta those ratty clothes and pick somethin' from the closet. We got some nice tees, crew neck sweaters, good jeans.

When we go to the Sandovals, we wanna look good."

Suddenly there was a knock on the door.

"Uh-oh!" Paul sighed with a grin. "Peace and quiet is over. My babe, Carmen, is here. I was wondering how long she could stay away once she knew you were home."

Paul swung open the door. "Come on in, doll," he said.

Once she planted a kiss on Paul, Carmen looked beyond him. "Hi, David!" she cried. She sprang across the room and gave David a big hug. "You look better already!" she commented. "You got more color in your face. But you're so skinny. You've got to eat a lot of nourishing food and build yourself up." She clasped his shoulders with both hands and held him at arm's length. "Oh, David," she remarked, "you look lots better than when Paul and I visited you the last time we went!"

"She's off and running," Paul declared.

Carmen ignored Paul. "Oh, David, isn't it wonderful what the boys did around here on Saturday? Your little room is so cozy. And is that a cool bed or what? That Ivan is such a sweetheart. My sister's so lucky to have a guy like him 'cause she's kind of a pill. I went shopping with Paul, and we got all your shampoo, toothpaste, soap, and stuff."

Carmen stepped back and looked David up and down. "Oh, David, you look just like Paul, only thinner. You guys are both so handsome. Wait a minute. Your eyes are a little lighter blue than Paul's, aren't they?"

"Prison pallor," Paul said drily. "His eyes faded too."

Carmen pushed Paul. "Oh, you! He does that all the time, David. He's just outrageous. You know what he said the other day? He said if I got interested in another guy, he'd take him out to the desert and stake him to an anthill!"

"I would too," Paul affirmed.

"Like I ever would dump Paul," Carmen responded. "I must be crazy to love him so much, but what can I do? Anyway, David, I'll be coming to the Sandovals with you and Paul on Sunday. I told Papa, and his mustache jumped several times.

"David, you are gonna love those Sandovals so much. Luis Sandoval, the father, he teaches history at Chavez, and he's the nicest man. He does so much for the kids. And Maria Sandoval, the mom, she's an angel. Then there's *Abuela* Lena, the cutest little old granny you'll ever meet. And Ernesto's two darling little sisters, and little Alfredo."

"Alfredo, he's the dude who's gonna give us trouble," Paul stated grimly.

Carmen gave Paul another shove. "Don't listen to him, David," she commanded. "Alfredo's a baby, and he's sooo cute. He's got these big dark eyes, he looks like a toy. And Abel Ruiz is doing the cooking. He's such a sweet guy, David, you'll love him. And you're gonna love whatever he cooks."

Paul looked at his brother. "She never stops talking," he remarked with a smirk on his face. "Sometimes she amazes me. She doesn't even have to breathe. If I didn't love the chick so much I would have stuffed a sock in her mouth months ago."

David smiled and laughed a little. "You're really pretty, Carmen," he noted.

"Oh, thank you, sir." Carmen made a little curtsey. "You know how Paul and I met? We were at Hortencia's taco place. I was driving the red convertible my father gave me for my birthday. Anyway, me and my stuffy sister Lourdes were going in. Suddenly somebody yells, 'Hey, homies, check out that red hot convertible.' Then he goes, 'Whoa, check out the chick at the wheel. She's even hotter.' I look, and there's these tough-looking dudes in hoodies, and they got tattoos. And I'm not used to stuff like that. I look at this dude I don't even know who's yelling so rudely at me. Then I almost drop dead because he is sooo handsome. And the hair is standing up on the nape of my neck and—"

Paul grabbed Carmen and kissed her on the mouth, shutting her off at midsentence. Paul turned and grinned at David. "It's the only way to stop her," he declared.

David actually laughed. He suddenly felt better about Sunday, now that he knew Carmen would be there. He made a mental note to sit close to her. As long as Carmen was talking—and she would be talking—maybe the others wouldn't notice him too much.

That night, David Morales couldn't quite believe where he was. He was lying in a nice, unbelievably comfortable bed, not a cot. The apartment had doors and windows, not bars. He was watching a movie on his own tiny television set, not staring at a concrete ceiling. He heard traffic sounds outside, not clanging steel doors or yelling and cursing. David wore earphones so that the sound of the movie wouldn't disturb Paul. His brother had to get up early and get to work managing an electronics store and then make classes at the community college.

David used to like crime dramas, but now he couldn't stand them. He didn't want to see anything that showed crime or cops chasing suspects down dark streets. He did like to watch reality singing competitions. He loved to watch dance shows too. He enjoyed funny movies with Adam Sandler and Will Ferrell. The movies were silly and bright and happy. They comforted him and helped to drive away the demons and the sickening memories of bars.

He liked the simple foolishness of the story lines. Their silliness helped him relax more than anything else. When he got too tired to watch the movies anymore, he drifted off into the best sleep he had enjoyed in more than two years.

In prison, David had never slept through the night. Men were shouting, coughing, rattling things. Guards were patrolling the corridors, checking steel doors. Some nights, sleep would be broken by brief, brutal incidents with curses and screams.

With the light out, now David could hear very different sounds in the dark. The snoring hisses of his sleeping brother. The long quavering screeches of the owl that lived in the gangly Washington palm tree in front of the apartment.

In the morning, Paul brewed coffee and poured raisin bran with milk.

"I better go looking for a job," David declared. "I want to get somethin' as quick as possible and pay my own way. You've done more than enough, Paul."

"That won't be easy, man," Paul remarked. "Lotta guys out there with no rap sheet looking for work."

"Remember the furniture store I worked at when you were going to Chavez?" David asked. "I did pretty good there. Mr. Hawthorne . . . do you think he's still there? He was a good guy. You see him lately?"

"Yeah, I see him sometimes," Paul replied. He had a funny look on his face.

"I worked hard there," David recalled. "Mr. Hawthorne told me I was the best kid he ever had. I started there when I was eighteen. I think you were livin' with the Baileys then. That was before you aged outta the system."

"Yeah," Paul recollected bitterly. "Old lady Bailey, she made me do the laundry. If her old man's socks weren't white enough, she'd slap me across the face. I was sure glad to get out of the foster care system."

The two young men silently stared at each other. Both were smirking. "Man," David finally said, "that system was like set up to break kids. It sure almost broke me."

"But it didn't," Paul asserted. Then he held up his hand for a fist-bump.

"Unbroken!" he declared.

David's face broke into a broad smile. "Unbroken!" he responded and fist-bumped with his brother.

David's thoughts then returned to finding a job.

"I worked for Mr. Hawthorne for about three and a half years," David was thinking out loud. "I think I'll go down there and see if he'd give me a chance. I never stole anythin' from him. I got in trouble after I quit there. I guess he probably knows what happened to me. I mean, it was all over the *barrio*. But he's gotta remember I was always on the up-and-up with him."

David looked at his brother. "I bet he'd give me a try, Paul. I always liked Mr. Hawthorne. Man, I'd really work hard. It's worth a try, don't you think, Paul?"

"Well, no harm in trying," Paul responded. "But don't get your hopes up too high. People change. Mr. Hawthorne isn't doin' as well as he was a coupla years ago. All the businesses up on Washington are having problems. But I'll drop you off on my way to work, and you can go talk to him."

"Thanks, Paul. I got a good feeling about this," David said. "If there's anybody who'd be willin' to give me a break, I think it'd be Mr. Hawthorne. He's gotta remember how hard I worked there, you know."

"If it doesn't work out, it's close enough for you to walk home, David," Paul told him.

As they left in the pickup, Paul advised his brother. "Lissen up, *hermano*, this isn't going to be any walk in the park. If you can't find anythin', I can help you."

"Paul, I'd never want you to get me in where you work," David objected. "That's a classy place with expensive electronics, just like the stuff I stole. I wouldn't wanna work at a place like that. And I surely wouldn't wanna damage your reputation where you got a good job by even asking for work."

"No, I wasn't thinking of my place," Paul replied. "They're not hiring anyhow. I got another little ace in the hole. So at the end of the week, if you've shaken a lotta trees and got no coconuts, we'll talk. It'd be in the restaurant business. Not a great job, but a place to start. So don't get discouraged. It's gonna be okay, man."

"I'm pretty sure Mr. Hawthorne will want me," David assured himself. "He knows what a good worker I was. Man, I'll break my back for him. But, thanks, Paul . . . for everything."

"The good thing about this job I'm thinking of, man," Paul added, "the owner of the place knows all about you. She'd hire you anyway. So there's light at the end of the tunnel. Okay?"

Paul pulled up to Hawthorne's furniture store and David got out. The boys high-fived each other and Paul declared, "It's gonna be okay, *hermano*. Trust me."

# CHAPTER TWO

The furniture store wasn't open yet. David remembered working at the place as a teenager. Mr. Hawthorne usually opened at ten, sometimes ten after ten. He was a middle-aged, heavyset man. He often complained of being tired and having sore feet.

That's why Mr. Hawthorne appreciated David so much while he worked here. He took a lot of the pressure off the man. Now David was prepared to work even harder. All he needed was for Mr. Hawthorne to give him a break. He needed to be hired for that all-important first job after being in prison. David knew he'd be deeply grateful to anybody who gave him a chance. He wouldn't let them down.

David looked through the window of the store. He saw the used and low-end new furniture—beds, sofas, chairs. The new furniture Mr. Hawthorne sold was called "stick furniture." It was poorly built, but it was all many people in the *barrio* could afford.

Suddenly the lights went on in the store. Mr. Hawthorne always came in the back door. David's heart began to race. He was sure Mr. Hawthorne would remember him. David began working here when he was barely eighteen and stayed at the store for quite some time. Mr. Hawthorne always complimented him a lot. David was hoping that the man would value David's past service enough that he could overlook his being in prison.

The "Closed" sign on the window was turned to "Open." Mr. Hawthorne swung open the front door and stood there for a second. He had put on at least fifty pounds. He looked like he'd aged a lot since David last saw him. David had changed too. He wondered whether his old boss would

23

remember him. David used to be a well-built, robust young man with longish curly black hair and bright eyes. Now he was much thinner, with a very short haircut and fear in the eyes that once sparkled with dreams.

"You're David Morales," Mr. Hawthorne remarked. "What are you doing here?" He sounded hostile. David's legs began to shake.

"I just wondered if you needed anybody, Mr. Hawthorne," David replied in a barely audible voice. "I need a job."

"I bet you do," the man snarled. "You wanna come in here and help yourself to my stuff. I heard you got out of prison. It makes me wanna puke. I don't believe in prisons."

The man almost turned away but swung back to face David. "I liked the way they did it in the Old West. Dirty thieving punks were hung from trees. Last year, a slimy creep come in here to rob me. He beat me so bad I was in the hospital for a week. Some mad dog posin' as a human being. You all oughta be in the grave."

"Mr. Hawthorne," David gasped, "I never hurt nobody. I never woulda done that to you. I'm sorry about what happened to you, but—"

"You're not sorry," Mr. Hawthorne snapped. "You're just sorry I ain't fool enough to hire you. You had me fooled before, Morales. I thought you were a straight-up kid. When I found out what you are, I swore I wouldn't even let you come in here. Not even as a customer."

"I never stole anything from you," David protested.

"I'm not so sure about that," the man growled. "I bet you stole plenty, but I was too stupid to catch you. I trusted you. Scum like you don't work nowhere without helping themselves when nobody's looking. Times when I couldn't get my books straight—you probably got in the cash drawer."

Mr. Hawthorne dismissed David with a wave of his hand. "Get outta my sight,

Morales. You'd be smart to get outta the *barrio*. Everybody knows what you are. Ain't nobody gonna want you. You're a dirty ex-con. Your kind doesn't reform. Once a criminal, always a criminal. Get off the sidewalk in front of my store and keep off, you hear me? Or I'll call the cops. You'll be back in the slammer before the sun goes down today."

David turned and hurried away. He really had hoped that Mr. Hawthorne might hire him, considering how hard he'd worked for him before. Even if he didn't get a job here, David figured, maybe he could get a letter of recommendation or something. He never thought he'd face such the bitter hatred. That shook him to his soul.

David got off Washington as fast as he could. Mr. Hawthorne's vindictive words kept running through his mind. They slashed at his heart like icy sleet during a blizzard. He felt so humiliated by the incident that he resolved not to tell anybody, not even Paul.

Two elderly women were coming in the opposite direction. They looked vaguely familiar to David. He couldn't place them, but he knew them from sometime in the past. They both looked at David, and he was sure he saw revulsion in their faces. Maybe he was just imagining things. But their faces seemed to tighten and grow hard. Their eyes narrowed, and they pressed shut their lips and hurried past him.

David hurried past the women and turned onto Polk. He just wanted to get back to the apartment and try to erase this morning from his mind. He didn't have the courage to look for work anywhere else right away. He was too bruised. His nerves were shattered.

David passed the Redbird Bar on Polk. He and his friends used to go in there even before they were of legal age. They used the drivers' licenses of older brothers or friends as ID. David remembered drinking a lot in that bar. The bar was where his troubles all

27

started. He started drinking too much and then using weed.

Sometimes they didn't have money to drink at the bar. David and his friends would boost cartons of beer and wine from the back of supermarkets. They'd go down to the ravine off Washington, to Turkey Neck, and drink until they passed out. A lot of homeless men and runaway kids hung out there too. Everybody usually got wasted at those parties.

"Davy!" somebody shouted as David passed the Redbird Bar. For a second, David froze in terror. He wasn't sure whether he was hearing the voice of another enemy or a friend. He didn't know whether he should turn or run for his life.

He turned and saw Freddy Meza, one of his old drinking buddies. Freddy was grinning and holding his arms open. He was about three years older than David. David had looked up to him in the old days as a very cool dude. "Davy," he exclaimed. "I heard you got out! Man, it is good to see you! You look like a ghost, Davy. Those slammers ain't no spas, right?"

Freddy hugged David and asked, "Where you livin' at, man? I could get a place for you. Me and a coupla guys—"

"No, thanks, Freddy," David interrupted. "I'm staying with my brother."

Freddy Meza continued grinning. "Paul always hated me, Davy. He's not like you. He's as mean as a snake. That tattoo on his hand fits him good. Paul's hardcore. Hey, Davy, come on in the bar. The drinks're on me. Augie's in there too. He'll freak when he sees you."

Augusto "Augie" Rojas was older than David too. He got David started burglarizing the stores at night. Augie and David were partners in crime, but Augie never got busted. David could have implicated Augie and turned state's evidence. His sentence would then have been a lot lighter, but he wouldn't drop a dime on Augie. He wouldn't rat him out, so David took the fall for both of them.

"I better not, Freddy," David responded.

"Come on, man," Freddy insisted, grabbing David's arm. "I told you I was buying." He dragged David into the bar and yelled to Augie, who was sitting on a stool. "Look what the cat dragged in, Augie! It's our old buddy, Davy Morales."

Augie had put on a lot of weight. He was almost thirty now. David was shocked to see him looking so different. But he had the same big smile. He hopped off his stool, rushed up to David, and embraced him. "Dude, you're solid gold," he cried emotionally. "They don't come any better." Augie always knew the kid had taken the rap for him. Augie already had a long rap sheet. If David had ratted him out, the conviction might have been a third strike for Augie. Augie was grateful.

"What'll you have, Davy?" Freddy asked. "Anything you want."

"I don't drink anymore," David declared.

"Are you kidding me, man?" Augie gasped. "You could hold your liquor better than any of us."

"Yeah, I know," David agreed. "My first run-in with the law was a DUI. I killed a palm tree. But in prison they had this program, and I ditched the booze. I committed to be sober, man. Besides, I'm on parole. I shouldn't even be in here. But I'll take a cup of coffee, though."

When David sat down, he asked, "So what are you guys up to now?"

"I got a gig as a messenger now, Davy," Augie answered. "I live in a dump with my chick, but you're welcome to crash there."

"I sell vacuum cleaners to old ladies," Freddy responded. "They'll buy anything just so somebody comes by and talks nice to them. They're so lonely. Their kids've dumped them, and mosta them're widowed. It's boring work, and half of them got dementia."

He grinned wickedly. "But there're fringe benefits. Last week some old bird, she reaches in her purse and wants to give me a tip. She thought she was giving me a ten, but it was a hundred! She didn't know

31

the difference. She kept hangin' onto my arm with her hand, all wrinkled like a little claw. I think she thought maybe I was her son or something." Freddy laughed.

David finished his coffee. A long time ago these were his best friends. He hung with them all the time. Paul was an angry teenager, just finishing at Cesar Chavez High. He told David his friends were pure trash. But David didn't want to hear that, especially from a brash kid brother. David had great times with Freddy and Augie, and they were all in the money from time to time. They could afford hot chicks, and life was good. Or so David thought.

"Well, I gotta be going," David announced. "It's been nice seeing you guys." He was lying, of course. Seeing them again wasn't nice at all. He didn't want to be with Freddy and Augie anymore. They were too much like the guys he had had to live with for the past two years. They were losers. They were bad news. They almost took David's whole life away.

As he walked back to the apartment, David Morales thought about that Sunday dinner at the Sandoval house. Did those people really want an ex-convict at their dinner table with their little kids and old grandmother? Paul had probably pushed the idea on Ernesto. And this Ernesto was a nice guy, so he gave in. That was how David saw it. Every time David thought about walking into that nice house with those good people, he got sick. In his mind, David saw Mr. Hawthorne's red, hate-filled face. He saw the angry, frightened looks on the faces of those old women on the street. He wondered whether Ernesto's father might feel the same way about ex-convicts. That was probably how the Sandoval grandma would look at him too.

When David got back to the apartment on Cardinal Street, he made himself some chicken noodle soup for lunch. Paul was due home around five, and David turned on the television. He half-watched a game. He used to enjoy football and baseball, but he hadn't kept up with the teams. He sat there like a zombie, not understanding who was who.

When David heard the doorknob turn, he stiffened. He turned off the TV and prepared to tell Paul that Mr. Hawthorne wasn't hiring.

"Hey, *hermano*, how you doin'?" Paul asked when he came in.

"Didn't get a job," David reported. "They don't need anybody at the furniture store."

"Okay, just a bump in the road. No problem. There'll be a job. Just take it easy, man," Paul assured him.

"Paul, I've been thinking about Sunday," David said. "You sure that's a good idea? I mean, this guy Ernie seems like such a good guy. Maybe he committed his parents to that dinner when they don't really want—"

"We're going," Paul declared. He pulled a ginger ale from the refrigerator and popped it open. "Don't sweat it, David. You'll love this family, and they'll love you. Be the best thing in the world for you. Hey, you remember Hortencia at the tamale shop, right? She's Ernesto's aunt. You and me used to go there."

"Yeah," David recalled. "Hortencia's pretty and nice. I used to stop in there sometimes after work at Hawthorne's."

"Remember me telling you I had an ace in the hole for you if nothin' else worked out, *hermano*?" Paul asked. "Well, Hortencia knows all about you, man, the whole *enchilada*. She said she'll hire you as counterman. Ernie texted me with that before you even got outta prison. I know it's not a great job, but it's something. Minimum wage and a cut of the tip jar."

Paul took a long slug from the soda can and went on. "And it beats sittin' around the house feeling sorry for yourself. But give it some time. You did a lotta college work, and there might be something real good out there for you. You got accounting classes and public relations under your belt. Who knows what might turn up? And if nothing does, then you can work at the tamale shop until you get your mojo back."

David sank bank in the leather chair, his brain spinning. He thought back to when he and Paul were little kids. Paul always had a dynamite personality. He'd flash that smile like a beam of light, and any darkness was gone. Paul found it easy to win friends. David wasn't like that. He was a shy kid. He took things harder. When the boys' mother died, David was twelve. Her death hit him harder than it did nine-year-old Paul. Even at nine, Paul seemed to understand that the pretty, troubled lady they called Mom was not Mom at all.

David remembered his mother's funeral on a cold January day. Mom looked beautiful in her coffin, as though she was only sleeping. The undertaker had done a wonderful job of covering up the ravages of drugs. David wept until his eyes ached. Paul never shed a tear.

After the funeral, social workers took custody of the two young boys in their shabby dark suits. There were no grandparents, no aunts or uncles, nobody. David remembered desperately hugging Paul before they went to separate foster homes. In some strange way, Paul seemed like the older of the two that day. He just kept saying to his older, taller brother, "Be okay. Be okay."

And Paul was still saying it, though David scarcely believed him anymore. On Sunday, David knew he would go to the Sandoval house with Paul. He'd go even though the thought of it horrified him.

On Saturday night, David couldn't sleep more than a few fitful naps. In the dark of the night, he pictured the Sandoval family standing at the door. His worst fears took shape in his mind. The father, a teacher at Cesar Chavez High, would be stern faced, as most of David's teachers had seemed to be. The mother would look distressed and frightened. To her, a pair of wolves were suddenly at their door and were going to come in. The grandmother would be leaning

37

on her cane. She'd be looking in dismay at her son and his wife, as if to ask them why they let such people in their home. The little girls would be hiding behind their mother, whimpering in fright, like kittens confronted by a fierce dog.

Ernesto, the do-gooder Paul always talked about, would be trying to put a good face on the awful situation. He would probably put on a fake smile and try to get his unhappy family to be welcoming. All of this ordeal would happen just because a worthless ex-convict happened to be Paul's brother.

On Sunday morning, after he showered and shaved, David put on a new green-striped polo shirt and jeans. It was part of the wardrobe Paul had bought for him and put into the closet before David got out of prison.

"You look good, man!" Paul declared. "Clothes are a little loose, but I didn't realize how thin you were. A few weeks from now, they'll fit you fine."

David climbed into the cab of the pickup truck that, years ago, was his. He had bought the pickup as his first vehicle, and he loved it. While David was in prison, Paul drove it. Now Paul drove down Tremayne Street toward the fateful dinner. They passed Bluebird Street and turned onto Wren.

David's heart was pounding. The palms of his hands were sweating. Paul turned into the driveway of the Sandoval house. David took in the pretty, well-kept yard and the nicely maintained house, with its fresh paint and nice drapes in the windows. It wasn't a big house, and nothing about it was elegant. But anyone could tell that a good family lived here. A police cruiser had never come here to collect a member of the Sandoval family.

David thought maybe he belonged with men like Freddy Meza and Augie Rojas, even though he wanted nothing to do with them. Surely, David thought, he didn't belong here on Wren Street.

# CHAPTER THREE

Carmen Ibarra's red convertible was already parked on the street. She had come early to help Abel prepare dinner. When Paul rang the doorbell, David wanted to spin around and run down the walk, then down the street. Perhaps he'd slow down in the next county.

But the door sprang open. There they were—Luis Sandoval and his wife, Maria, both of them smiling. In front of them were two little girls with huge eyes and lustrous black hair. Big grins brightened their faces.

Before anybody else had a chance to say anything, Katalina Sandoval began chattering. "Hi, Paul! Hi, David! I'm Katalina, and I'm the oldest girl. You look just like Paul,

David, only skinnier. Do you have tattoos? Paul has this cool tattoo of a rattlesnake that jumps when he makes a fist!"

Not to be outdone, Juanita piped up. "Do you like *The Flintstones*? I love *The Flintstones*. I like it when Fred goes yabba-dabba do. But *Abuela* says they're real old. They were on the TV when she was young. But I love the old reruns, David."

David stared at the two little girls for a second. He seemed to be running something through his mind. Mom and Dad stared blankly at the girls. They'd planned a different greeting, but the girls seemed to have things over. Then David finally spoke.

"Let's see. Hi, Katalina. No, no tattoos. Hi, Juanita. Yes, I loved the Flintstones when I was little. They were reruns even then. Sometimes I wished Fred Flintstone was my dad."

Juanita giggled. "I wouldn't want Fred Flintstone as my dad. He'd come to school and meet my teacher in those funny clothes."

41

Luis Sandoval finally grabbed David's hand and greeted him. "Well, welcome, David. This is my wife, Maria. You've got to excuse my girls. They just love visitors."

"Hi, David," Maria Sandoval said, clearing a path for Paul and David. "It's a pleasure to meet you. Paul has said wonderful things about you."

Then, in her best "mom" voice, she commanded, "Come on girls, help Abel and Carmen set the table. The boys are hungry." The aroma of *carne asada* filled the little house.

Ernesto appeared from the hallway and introduced himself and *Abuela*. The two young men shook hands and exchanged greetings. The grandmother smiled at David and remarked, "You've got nice blue eyes like Paul."

On the way to the table, David studied Ernesto. He was a handsome young man. He looked perfect. David thought he probably *was* perfect. He had to be every mother's dream of what a son should be.

Fortunately, David thought, he never disappointed his own mother. She had disappointed him enough and didn't live long enough for him to disappoint her.

Katalina put herself between Paul and David. "Paul," she commanded, "make a fist! I wanna see the snake on your hand jump!"

Paul obliged by placing his fist close to the little girl's face and squeezing his hand hard. The snake jumped, and the little girl screamed in delight.

As people took their seats, David forgot all about sitting next to Carmen. He felt a lot better about how things would go down.

Abel then appeared with Carmen, bringing the appetizer. It was *rum chica rum* chicken. It was chicken breast, marinated in orange, rum, and spices. Then it was grilled and cut into very thin slices. Able served it with a thickened version of the marinade and garnished with thin orange slices. They placed the plates in front of everyone and then sat down.

"Wow!" Ernesto exclaimed as he took his first bite. "Abel, dude, slow down! It's gonna be hard to top this."

Paul picked up Ernesto's remark. "Here's the dude who's gonna rule the Internet as the chef of the century in a few years. Abel Ruiz, best cook on the planet. And by his side, the hottest nonstop-talking chick who sometimes takes a breath."

The table talk was on.

"My teachers say I talk too much, too, Carmen," Katalina chirped. "I've got Ms. Corona this year, and she's really mean. She says she wishes it was the old days when teachers were allowed to put tape on their students' mouths."

Carmen poked Paul in the shoulder. "He's always dissing me about how much I talk, David. And he's a worse big mouth than me."

"Yeah, I guess I do talk too," Paul admitted. "I had one of those mean teachers in fourth grade, Kat. Remember, David, what I did?"

David smirked as he recalled. It was the last year their mother was alive. They all lived together in a ratty little bungalow. As bad as things were, that year was the last good one David remembered.

"Yeah," David chuckled, "Paul had this pet tarantula. So he brought it to school and stuck it on the teacher's desk when she was writing on the blackboard. She ran screaming out of the room."

Katalina and Juanita both screeched in delight. "What happened? What happened, Paul?" Juanita demanded. "Did you get busted?"

Paul laughed and David went on. "Paul sneaked the tarantula back in his box and hid it in his book bag. When the teacher came running back with the principal, there was Paul, as innocent as a lamb, saying the teacher just imagined the whole thing. They couldn't prove anything, so all Paul got was a scolding from the principal."

"Ooh, tarantulas are so spooky," Katalina remarked. "They got furry bodies. Paul, was the tarantula really your pet?"

"Sure," Paul replied. "I named him Theodore."

Ernesto was quiet until this point, busy with his appetizer. Now he spoke up. "David, I had a pet chuckwalla when I was in fourth grade. Remember, Mom?"

"Don't remind me!" Maria Sandoval groaned with a wry grin. "It was such a horrible-looking creature. Luckily it didn't eat live food like most lizards. It lived on flowers and cactus."

"Then my chuckwalla ran away, and I felt really bad," Ernesto continued, with a wicked grin. "It was a tragedy."

"Yes," Ernesto's father added, "especially for the rest of us because it was loose somewhere in our house. They hide in crevices, and your mother wouldn't even go to bed until we found it."

"*After three days!*" Mom wailed.

*Abuela* Sandoval was not looking critically at David, as he thought she would. She was a kindly looking elderly woman, darker than her son, Luis. She joined the conversation, perhaps to fill the lull. She turned to David and commented, "My father's name was David too. David Franco. It's a fine, strong name, David."

David smiled at the woman. "Thanks. I like it too," he responded.

"Yes," Paul agreed. "I always used to tell David when we were kids what to do if we ever ran into a bully. He hadda go get a slingshot, find a nice round stone, and put it right between the dude's eyes. You know, like David in the Bible did to Goliath."

Abel and Carmen rose from the table, and people started handing their dishes down to them. The pair disappeared into the kitchen. After a few minutes, they came out again with plates of *carne asada*. It was wrapped up in a flour tortilla with a great-looking salsa and avocado slices.

As everybody started eating dinner, compliments rained down on Abel. "Man," Paul remarked, "this is the best *carne asada* I ever tasted."

"Did you take a lot of cooking lessons, Abel?" David asked. "This is a wonderful meal."

"No," Abel responded. "I just listen to the chefs on TV and read a lot of books and stuff. I practice and practice. When I finish at Chavez, I'm goin' to culinary school."

Then Abel asked, "How about you, David? Paul said you took a lotta classes in accounting and public relations and stuff. What would you like to do?"

"Soon's I got a job nailed down," David answered, "I'm going to the community college for more credits. I'll probably go nights. But I'm not sure what I want to do . . ."

Luis Sandoval spoke up. "They've got good counselors at the college, David. They can find your strengths and steer you in the right direction. When you get your

48

associate in arts degree, you can transfer to the state university. I do some teaching at community. Stay in touch with me. I can help you when you're ready."

"Thanks!" David responded. "I will."

David was starting to feel almost normal, like part of the human race. He was just a young guy having dinner with his brother's friends. They didn't look down at him at all because he'd been in prison. For the first time since he walked through those prison gates, David Morales had a new take on his future. Maybe, he thought, he *did* have a chance to fit in somewhere. The florid, hate-filled face of Mr. Hawthorne faded a little.

The conversation also faded as people dug into their *carne asada* and went for seconds. Abel beamed. When the table talk stops, he always figured, the food was good.

After dinner, the women were busy in the kitchen. They had agreed to be the cleanup crew. Ernesto, Paul, Abel, and David went out to shoot baskets at the hoop on the garage door. Then they sprawled in lawn chairs with chilled sodas.

"David, Paul told you about Hortencia's offer, right?" Ernesto asked.

"Yeah, that was pretty awesome," David replied.

"*Tía* Hortencia is something else," Ernesto said.

"It's good to know there's something to fall back on if I can't come up with something on my own," David remarked. He swallowed hard. The elephant was in the living room: Nobody wanted to mention David's past. But he figured it was time. "I don't have a real good résumé, you know."

"You can say that again," Paul laughed.

Abel shook his head. "You couldn't have a worse time getting a job than I did, David. I looked and looked. I have a sort of dorky personality, and nobody would hire me. Then I got this job at Elena's doughnut shop." Abel frowned. "What a bummer that was."

"Yeah," Paul added. "I worked there too. This crazy lady kept missing money and blamin' us, especially me. She wanted to do strip searches. She figured I was the most likely thief. She liked Abel, but I was the dude who probably stole the money. She didn't even know about my brother in the slammer, or my goose woulda really been cooked."

David found himself laughing at that. He was at ease with all the people at the table.

"Uh-oh!" Paul said suddenly. "Here she comes, Miss Mouth."

Carmen let the door slam behind her as she came out. "I heard that!" she announced.

She sat down next to Paul and quickly ran her fingers through his thick, glossy hair. "Good thing this dude is so hot, or I woulda dumped him months ago," she told everyone. Then she looked at David, "Let your hair grow, David. You've got amazing hair like Paul, and girls like it long."

51

David turned to Ernesto. "Man, you got a great family, Ernie. Your parents are so nice. Your grandma and those little girls, they just melt a guy's heart," he commented.

"Thanks," Ernesto said. "But I didn't do anything to deserve them. It just happens."

"Yep," Abel agreed. "The old stork drops you on a doorstep. If the wicked witch of the west lives there, you're screwed. She picks you up and sweeps you into her domain with her bosom."

"Abel," Ernesto scolded, "it's not that bad with you. Come on."

Abel turned to David. "Picture this, dude. You got a brother who is handsome, brilliant, charming, the apple of his adoring mother's eye. Right now he's in college earning straight As. He's got so many chicks coming after him that he has to beat them off with a stick."

Abel grinned at everyone and then went on. "Then there's me. This morning I overheard Mom talking to Dad. Not really talking *with* him, but *at* him. Dad might as well be a ventriloquist's dummy. He moves his lips, and Mom's voice comes outta his mouth. Anyway, Mom thinks I'm still in bed, so she's talking freely. She goes, 'Sal, how can they be brothers? Tomás just texted me. He's got the highest GPA in his class. And he's going with this lovely girl whose father is an ambassador to some little country—I forget the name of it.' "

Paul, David, and Ernesto started laughing. Abel continued in a grim voice, even though he was making fun. "And then Mom goes, 'Poor Abel, barely clinging to a C at Chavez. Then the girl he loved with all his heart and soul just dumped him for a nobody. Claudia wasn't much to begin with, but at least she was a decent-looking girl. I thought it was a miracle that she found Abel attractive, and then—' "

"Oh, Abel!" Carmen scoffed. "It can't be that bad. Your mom loves you and that's worth a lot."

"I hear you, man," Paul chimed in, ignoring Carmen. "But look at it this way. Ten years from now, you'll be a top chef, raking in the money. The chicks'll be yowlin' at your door like kitties after the hottest tom on the fence. And old Tomás'll be married to this chick whose father is ambassador to Transylvania. Then he'll find out she's Dracula's daughter when she starts nipping at his neck."

David started laughing again. He couldn't remember laughing this hard in years. It felt good to be just hanging out with good friends. It felt good to be accepted.

Later, when David and Paul were headed home in the pickup, Paul spoke to his brother. "Didn't I tell you it'd be great, *hermano*?"

"Yeah, you did," David admitted. "Being in prison makes a guy jumpy, nervous. You don't expect much. When you've been locked up with some really bad dudes, you find it hard to believe there are people in the world like them. Like the Sandovals and Abel."

When they pulled up to the apartment parking lot on Cardinal Street, two men were just leaving the apartment building. Paul's happy expression instantly turned venomous. He recognized Freddy Meza and Augie Rojas. The two men recognized Paul and David, and they started walking toward the car.

"What do you guys want?" Paul yelled in a hostile voice.

"Augie and me just wondered if our old friend wanted to shoot some pool," Freddy shouted back.

"Yeah," Augie added, "we all were at the Redbird Bar over on Polk. And he told us he was living here since he got out."

"Dudes," Paul snarled savagely, "don't *ever* come back here again. Don't go near my brother, you understand? I'm not kidding. He's been through a hard time, and he's puttin' his life back together again. He doesn't need rats like you messing with his head? Stay away from him and from here if you want to stay healthy. Y'hear?"

"Hey, we didn't mean anything," Augie responded, holding his hands up as a peace signal. He glanced over at David. "Your brother talkin' for you too, Davy?"

David felt humiliated. He nodded and spoke in a low voice. "Yeah." He looked down at the ground as he spoke.

"He your parole officer now, Davy?" Freddy asked in a growl. "He callin' all the shots?"

"Get lost, or you'll be sorry you were ever born," Paul threatened. At that, the two men walked away.

Paul went into the apartment after David. He threw his keys down on the kitchen table, and they landed with a loud clatter. Paul commented in a sarcastic voice, "I guess I got no right to know you been hangin' with the creeps. Those are the idiots who got you in trouble in the first place. I guess that's none of my business."

"Paul," David explained, "after I went looking for a job at Hawthorne's, they came out of the Redbird Bar. I was passing by, and they started talking. Okay, I went in the bar with them and had a cup of coffee. That's all."

David stood in the living room, facing Paul and his back to the sofa. Paul came at him and gave him a violent shove, knocking him backward onto the sofa cushions.

"Tell me the whole friggin' truth, and tell me now," Paul demanded.

"They offered to buy me drinks," David explained. "I said I'd quit liquor. I had a cup of coffee, and we talked maybe for five minutes. That's all it was."

"You shouldna gone into that bar with them, you fool," Paul yelled. "Don't you remember it was Augie Rojas who got you into busting in stores and boosting stuff? You forget about that? He was older than you, and he got you heisting the stuff. Then he sold it. When you got busted, the cops knew you weren't operatin' on your own. You got the chance to tell them what that snake did, roping a fool kid into his dirty business. But you saved Augie's backside and kept your mouth shut."

Paul was so angry; he flapped his arms in the air once or twice. Then he stomped around the room in frustration. When he spoke again, he was nearly shouting. "You did hard time because of him. Okay, I can understand you not wantin' to rat the guy out, though I would have in your place. But after all you been through, after all *we* been through, you're stupid enough to go in a bar and sit with those cockroaches. I can't believe this. Talk to me, man. Make me understand how you could be so stupid. Help me make sense of a guy who hasn't been out of the slammer for a whole day. Then he goes in a bar to shoot the breeze with a couple of creeps who derailed his whole life."

David felt terrible. Getting such a dressing-down from his kid brother made him feel small and humiliated. Shame swept over him like a tidal wave, drowning his self-respect. Finally his voice came, slowly and sadly.

"I'm sorry, Paul," he murmured. "That day . . . Mr. Hawthorne, he didn't just tell me he had no openin' at the store. He screamed at me. Said I was no good and I'd never be any good. He said I was a criminal. My only hope was to get as far away from the *barrio* as I could. He said nobody would give me a chance . . . nobody. Then I was walking away from there. I felt like the whole world was starin' me down."

David was slumped on the couch, his head down, as he spoke. "I was passin' the Redbird Bar, and I heard a friendly voice yell my name. I turned to go, but he grabbed my arm and almost pulled me into the place. I was so desperate and depressed. I lost my head, and I went in there for five minutes to talk to Freddy and Augie. It was stupid. I know that. I don't blame you for being mad."

As much as Paul had hurt him, he understood his kid brother's rage and bewilderment. David knew he had to take whatever Paul dished out. He deserved it. Paul Morales had come to that prison regularly to visit him, to cheer him up, to give him hope when he had very little hope.

When he first arrived at the prison, David had given up hope of ever having a decent life again. Paul's visits were a lifeline. They were the only glimmer of light at the end of the darkest tunnel David had ever seen.

Now, Paul and his friends had embraced him. They welcomed him back into their world as though he were worth saving. Paul was giving him a home and support. Paul introduced him to his friends, who were good, decent people.

"I'm sorry, Paul. It won't ever happen again," David promised quietly. "If I see those guys on the street, I'll act like I never seen them before. I swear to you on my life."

Paul sat down on the sofa next to his brother. He threw his arm around David's shoulders. "Okay," was all he said. That was the end of it.

Paul glanced around the room, as if trying to think of something else to say. Finally, he spoke. "Any good movies on? Wanna watch one?"

"Yeah," David responded.

Paul grabbed the remote control for the TV and started clicking toward the movie channel.

# CHAPTER FOUR

The next morning, after Paul Morales left for work, David walked up Washington Street. The street had a lot of fast-food places, thrift stores, ninety-nine-cent stores. A couple of them had "Help Wanted" signs in the window. David noticed such a sign at the yogurt shop, and he went in.

David had showered, put on a good deodorant, shaved and dressed in a clean shirt and jeans. When he looked in the mirror before leaving the apartment, he saw a presentable-looking guy. But there was a haunted look in his eyes. Maybe, he thought, no one would notice.

The past two years had taken their toll. A feeling nagged him. He felt

unemployable except through the kind-
ness of friends who would reluctantly let
him work. He wanted so much to get that
first job. He'd pick up garbage or clean
the gutters if that was what it took. He just
wanted a chance, and he was terrified that
he wouldn't get it.

"Hi," David said to a middle-aged La-
tina woman in the yogurt shop. "I saw your
sign, and . . . uh . . . I'm looking for a job."

The woman looked David over. He
thought her expression was not too invit-
ing, but maybe his imagination was at work
again. She dug into a drawer and brought
out an application. "Here, take a seat in one
of the booths and make this out. Give it to
me when you're done."

David took the application and sat
down. He began filling out his name, address, phone number, and other information with a ballpoint pen. He said that he
graduated from Canoga Park High School.
He had about two years of junior college
but no degree. He didn't indicate where

he got the college credits. Then David got to the question that sent chills up his spine.

"Have you ever been arrested and convicted of a crime?" There were several lines to explain if the answer was yes.

You weren't supposed to lie on job applications. David's parole officer told him to tell the truth. The man said to explain the circumstances as honestly as he could. But honesty didn't make sense to David. If he admitted he was sent to prison for felony burglary, who'd want him? A lot of young guys with clean records were finding it hard to get jobs.

David lied. He wrote no to the question. He hoped against hope they wouldn't check. He figured he had no chance at all if he was honest. By lying, he had a slim chance if they didn't do a check.

David returned the completed application to the lady.

"You put your cell phone number down too?" she asked in a disinterested voice.

"Yes," David replied. Paul had given him an inexpensive cell phone. His brother had seen to everything.

The woman tucked the application into a space behind the counter and said nothing. "I'd really appreciate it if you'd consider me," David added.

"It's not up to me," the woman explained. She never made eye contact as she spoke. "The boss comes in later and looks the applications over. He'll call you for a personal interview if he's interested."

"How soon . . . usually does it take?" David asked. "You know . . . to find out if there'll be an interview?"

The woman shrugged.

"Thanks," David said, leaving the yogurt shop. He had little hope, very little hope. Maybe the lady had enough street smarts to recognize David's prison pallor. Maybe she just didn't like the looks of him. Maybe she even knew who he was.

David didn't put in any other applications. His spirits had sunk too low. He thought, "What if I *never* get a job? What if that Hortencia changes her mind about taking me on? I can't sponge off my brother forever. I can't eat the food he buys and use the utilities. I've caused him enough trouble."

David decided to take off if he didn't find work. He'd just pack up his few belongings when Paul was gone to work and go away. He'd have to do it while Paul was away. Paul'd never let him go if he was there. David thought he soon wouldn't have any self-respect left at all. He'd prefer living on the street with the other homeless down-and-outers than being a permanent burden on his kid brother.

As David walked, his cell phone rang.

"Yeah?" David said, a tiny ember of hope glowing in him. Maybe that mean-looking lady didn't dislike him after all. Maybe she talked the boss at the yogurt shop into giving him an interview.

But it was Carmen. "David, is it okay if I come over to your place this afternoon after school?" she asked.

"Sure," David responded. "Paul usually gets home a little after five."

"I want to talk to you, not Paul," Carmen explained.

"Oh," David said. "Okay." He returned the phone to his pocket. New fears arose in him, clawing at his insides.

David could see how much Carmen Ibarra loved Paul. Maybe, David worried, she resented David being around. Maybe Carmen didn't like Paul's ex-convict brother living at the apartment and dragging Paul down. She acted as though she liked David at the dinner at the Sandovals, but maybe she was having second thoughts. David made up his mind. If Carmen expressed any misgivings about him living here, he'd take off right away. Paul and Carmen had a good thing going. David didn't want to spoil things for Paul. He'd hurt the kid enough already.

The school day at Cesar Chavez High was over at three-thirty. Carmen pulled her red convertible into the lot on Cardinal

Street at four. Even before she rang the bell, David opened the door. He had prepared himself for something bad to happen. "Hi, Carmen," David said. "Come on in."

"Thanks, David," she said. She was wearing a hot pink sweater that emphasized her lovely figure. "How're you doin'?"

"Uh, okay," David answered grimly. He wasn't going to share his misery with her.

"You find a job yet?" Carmen asked.

"I . . . uh . . . put in some applications and stuff," David responded. His suspicion grew that she was troubled by his being here. She was probably looking for a nice way to tell him it was time to move on.

Carmen sat down on the living room sofa. She patted the cushion next to her as a sign that David should join her. When both were seated on the couch, Carmen said what she wanted to say.

"David, you know that Paul and I are nuts about each other. I mean, Paul's nuts anyway, but he loves me. That's the best thing that's ever happened to me. I mean,

I look okay and all that, but I'm not drop-dead gorgeous like some of the girls at Chavez. I mean, like you take for example Naomi Martinez, Ernie's girl. She is sooo pretty. But Paul thinks I'm hot, and I *know* he's hot. I'm just so incredibly happy with him. But there's this one problem."

"Here it comes," David thought, steeling himself.

"David, my father," Carmen went on, "you know, the councilman, Emilio Zapata Ibarra. He's the most wonderful dad a girl ever had. I love him so much. I love both my parents. But, well, he has misgivings about Paul. He never wanted me to date Paul in the first place. When he first met Paul and saw the rattlesnake tattoo on his hand, he like went ballistic. Well, my father's sort of hot tempered anyway, and you and I both know that Paul can be explosive. Well . . . the thing is . . . Dad wanted me to date Ernesto Sandoval, but that didn't work out. Ernie was madly in love with Naomi. No way was that gonna happen."

David's brain began to malfunction. Paul had told him that nobody in the world could talk as much as Carmen. Now, after a few minutes of listening to her, David had no idea what she was trying to say. As she chattered on, David tried to smile and nod from time to time.

"Well," Carmen continued, "when I met Paul and we started going together, I never knew I could be so happy. He's like my whole life. But I want Mama and Daddy to be happy too. Well, my father knows you just got out of prison. As you can imagine, he's a little nervous. He didn't say that, but I can tell. He said he wants to meet you as soon as possible."

"What?" David gasped.

"Yes, tonight," Carmen affirmed. "Papa wants you to come to our house for cake and coffee. Mama made a maple cake with cream cheese frosting, and it's so good. Paul can come too. It's very important, David. Papa isn't crazy about Paul anyway. You've got to come and reassure my parents that you're, you know, not like Paul. I have a lot of trouble calming my parents down, especially my father. He knows Paul hangs out with guys like Cruz and Beto, and they have this crazy van covered with wild pictures.

"Well, David, I gotta go home," Carmen declared, shifting forward on the sofa. "So the thing is, my father wants you there at seven tonight. You and Paul. We live on Nuthatch Lane. Paul knows our house, of course. He's made some crude comments about where we live—you know, Nuthatch Lane—but, thankfully, not in front of my father. Remember, seven!"

"Okay," David agreed meekly.

Carmen paused. She looked intently at David and then spoke. "You're a lot different from Paul, David. I love Paul madly. But if he was just a teeny tiny bit more like you, it'd be going better with my parents."

"Well," David muttered. He raised one hand in a what-can-I-say? gesture. It was all he could manage.

"Thanks for listening to me, David," Carmen went on. Before she got up from the sofa, she planted a kiss on David's cheek. Then she jumped up and said, "Remember, seven sharp. Dad's a bug on punctuality."

When Paul got home, David reported in a flat voice, "Carmen was here." During the past hour, David had been going over and over in his mind how tonight would go. This Councilman Ibarra was the guy with the mustache that jumped when he was angry. Was he going to inspect David like meat? Was he going to judge whether David Morales was fit to be the brother of his daughter's boyfriend?

Paul hung up his jacket. "Oh yeah? What'd she want?"

"We have to go to her house at seven tonight for maple cake and coffee," David explained. "Her father wants to meet me. I guess he thinks I'm some kind of an ax murderer or something. I'm sick about it. I don't want to ruin things for you, Paul."

Paul laughed. "Don't sweat it, man. He couldn't hate you more than he hates me. The guy's tried everything under the sun to drive me away, but I'll never go. He had this fantasy of Carmen falling for Ernie, the goody-two-shoes dude. The poor old guy almost split a gut when Carmen and I got together. When Carmen's sister, Lourdes, first saw me, she almost called the cops. Don't worry about it, man. We'll go over there, eat some cake, drink some coffee, and cut out as fast as we can."

"I just don't want to make it harder for you," David said.

"*Hermano*," Paul told him, "you're my blood. You go with the territory. You're part of me, maybe the better part."

At six thirty, Paul and David climbed into the pickup and drove to Nuthatch Lane. "David," Paul advised, "don't expect this dude, Mr. Ibarra, to be like Luis Sandoval. He's gonna be blunt. When we were at the Sandovals, nobody mentioned anythin' about you being in the slammer. It won't be like that with Mr. Ibarra. He'll want to ask questions. Just be honest. I don't have to tell you that, though. You got much better manners than I do."

The moment the boys were at the front door, Carmen opened it. She must have been watching from the window. "Hi, guys," she greeted. Then she turned toward the interior of the house and yelled, "They're here!"

"Oh man!" David muttered under his breath.

Paul reached over and punched his brother's shoulder. "Don't sweat it, dude. It'll be fine," he assured his brother.

David spotted Emilio Zapata Ibarra the moment he entered the house. He was a tall, swarthy man with a huge, great drooping mustache. He looked like a giant walrus. Under the mustache were large white teeth. "Like a crocodile," David thought. The man had flashing dark eyes. To David, his smile seemed more like an angry sneer.

"Hello, Paul and David," Mr. Ibarra boomed. "You must be David!" He charged forward. For just one terrible split second, David thought he would seize him and throw him out the front door. Instead, he grabbed David's hand in a powerful grip that seemed capable of breaking all of David's fingers but somehow didn't.

Mr. Ibarra's wife, Conchita emerged from the kitchen door. She was a pretty, slightly plump woman in a flaming red dress. She wore bright red lipstick, and she looked like a showgirl. "I made a maple cake with cheesecake frosting," she cried in a loud voice. "Come on into the parlor."

David finished the sentence in his mind: ". . . said the spider to the fly."

David glanced at Paul, who was grinning. He was used to all this. Sensing his nervousness, Carmen leaned over to David. She whispered, "Papa just wants to get to know you, David. Don't be nervous."

They all sat down in velvety chairs in the living room, and Conchita went to get the cake and coffee. Mr. Ibarra's gaze lasered in on David. In his booming voice, he asked, "So you just got out of prison, eh, David?"

"Yes," David gasped. He longed for the maple cake and the moment Mr. Ibarra would take a bite and be unable to speak.

"You were a burglar, as I understand it," Mr. Ibarra went on. He said it in the same tone of voice he might have used to say, "You were an electrician, eh?"

Conchita entered the room with the maple cake, followed by Carmen with plates and cutlery. Conchita set the lovely cake on the table. Then she brought the coffee while Carmen followed her with cups, sugar, and cream. "Here we are!" Conchita Ibarra sang out gaily.

Emilio Ibarra had been brutally blunt. As David took a cup of coffee—black—from Carmen, he finally stammered, "Yes, I was a burglar." He took a quick swallow of coffee. Carmen deftly cut the cake and put a generous slice on each plate. David thought he might upchuck if he ate any cake, but he had no choice.

"But now you're out, and all that is behind you," Mr. Ibarra continued, smiling
with his big teeth. He dove into the maple
cake with gusto, crying, "Ah, Conchita,
magnificent as usual! The cheesecake frosting is marvelous!"

When Mr. Ibarra had finished his first
bite, he returned his attention to David.
"Now you are on parole, is that right?" he
asked. "That's to be expected. It is very important to keep all your appointments with
the parole officer. Those fellows can be
your best friend while you are adjusting to
life on the outside."

Paul rolled his eyes, and Carmen kicked
him. But Mr. Ibarra didn't notice them. He
was too focused on David. David felt like
a bug in a display case. Mr. Ibarra was the
scientist holding him firmly with a giant pin.

"Have some of the maple cake, David,"
Conchita suggested. "You're too thin." Her
urging sounded like an order. David took a
small bite and it was delicious. But he was
too intimidated to appreciate it.

"As you surely know," Mr. Ibarra stated, no longer smiling, "Paul and my daughter are very good friends."

"That's putting it mildly," Paul muttered under his breath. But Mr. Ibarra had excellent hearing. He looked at Paul with a baleful eye, then turned to David. "Your brother is a master of sarcasm."

David didn't know what to say, so he quickly grabbed another bite of the maple cake. He was waiting for some hard verbal blow from the mustached man. He was waiting to hear some damning comment. In his mind, he could almost hear what the man would say.

"David Morales, you are a foul criminal. You broke the laws of this great republic, in which I am honored to serve as a councilman. You sneaked into business establishments and stole what was not yours. You wanted only to enrich your miserable self. Yes, you are now out of prison. But the crimes you've committed have tarnished your soul for all time. You shall never be welcome in my home or in decent society."

Instead, Mr. Ibarra leaned forward and asked, "Tell me, David, what did you learn in prison?" He was closer to David now and even more frightening. The big mustache danced. "Carmen said you studied accounting and had other classes too. Tell me about that."

"Uh . . . public relations and stuff," David gasped.

"What did you get out of the experience of being in prison, David?" Mr. Ibarra continued. His big black eyes seemed to grow larger and more malevolent.

David's thoughts swirled like a tornado. He wished he were eloquent enough to say something profound. Within those dark, dank prison walls, had he grasped the meaning of life? Would he use some newfound, hard-won wisdom to become a great person and an asset to humanity?

But all David could do was glance at Paul, who looked annoyingly amused as he stuffed maple cake in his mouth. He looked over at Carmen, who looked lovingly into Paul's eyes. All she cared about was her own romance. All David could do was stare at Mr. Ibarra. His great mustache quivered and danced, and his eyes grew ever larger and more demanding.

"Perhaps I'm not phrasing my question clearly. What do you think was the most important lesson you learned in prison, David?" Mr. Ibarra's tone was now more demanding. Where was the councilman going with these questions, David wondered?

# CHAPTER FIVE

I learned to keep my head down so the other guys wouldn't kill me," David answered finally.

Emilio Zapata Ibarra continued to look at David for a moment. Then he threw his head back and roared with laughter. "David," he inquired, "did you get into any fights in prison?"

"No," David replied promptly. He put two hands up, palms out. "Never." In fact, David was so good at avoiding trouble that the prison authorities often paired him with troublesome inmates. David never had a problem with them. Nothing could provoke him.

"Ah," Mr. Ibarra concluded. "So you are good at getting along with people, eh? All kinds of people?"

At this point, Paul Morales was beginning to look puzzled. He even stopped eating his large slice of cake. Why did Carmen's father want to meet David? Carmen was bewildered too. She assumed her parents just needed some reassurance about David. They wanted to be sure that he was a decent, nonviolent young man who'd made a mistake and was now reformed. That was all anybody thought was going on.

"So, David," Mr. Ibarra went on, "have you found a job yet?"

"Not yet, but I'm looking hard," David answered. "I filled in an application at this yogurt shop, but I haven't heard yet. Somebody said they were hiring down at the car wash at the end of Washington. I'll try there tomorrow."

Mr. Ibarra leaned back in his chair and clasped his hands thoughtfully behind his head. "You are not who I expected you to be, David," he remarked.

David said nothing. He wondered where he'd failed to make a good impression. He had certainly tried.

The big man continued, his mustache twitching for emphasis at certain words. "It is no secret that I have had some disagreements with your brother. He has, shall we say, a volatile personality. I am not criticizing him, mind you. He is a fine young man. But it would be nice if he did not have a rattlesnake tattoo on his hand. It would also be nice if he did not ride in cars that jump up and down in the street or drive a graffiti-scarred van."

Mr. Ibarra nodded toward Paul. "Nevertheless," he went on, "my most precious, beloved daughter cares deeply for your brother. I must respect that. Tonight I was expecting you to be very much like Paul, though I'd hoped you'd lack some of his mercurial qualities. I am delighted to see that you are much calmer and more, shall we say, even tempered."

Both Paul and Carmen were now dumbfounded. They stared at Mr. Ibarra in silence.

"David," Mr. Ibarra stated, "as you know, I'm a member of the city council. It is a job for which I worked long and hard for. I was grateful to be elected, and I am trying desperately to meet the needs of the constituents. Sadly, the political scene is now an angry and often bitter place. Men and women, frustrated in their lives, vent their rage against elected officials. In my office, I have a lovely woman who has been bravely fending off the clamoring mob. A young man is doing the same, but they both are nearing nervous breakdowns from the vitriol of some constituents. Constituents call to accuse me of stealing from the city. Irate citizens threaten to shove me and my staff into potholes if we don't get them filled quickly enough."

The councilman sighed deeply. "So, David, the bottom line is that I have an opening on my staff. I need some brave soul with the patience of that Biblical fellow Job. He also must have the stamina to help me survive this monstrous job I have gotten myself into."

A total dead silence fell on the room. Paul's eyes widened. When he opened his mouth to speak, nothing came out. Carmen, never at a loss for words, was also speechless.

David looked at the man with the great mustache and the shining white teeth. He asked softly, "Are you talking about a job, Mr. Ibarra?"

"David, you have survived the crucible of prison," Emilio Ibarra responded. "Unlike Paul, you have the skills to create harmony out of madness. There is a gentle spirit about you that is warmly comforting. All you need to do is be polite and take the abusive phone calls without answering in kind. Just soothe peoples' feelings. Try to solve the problems that are solvable. And try to convince others that a city councilman is not the Almighty who can fix everything.

If you would like to try to do that, then I will put you on my staff."

David stood up and declared in a voice thick with emotion, "Thank you, Mr. Ibarra. I promise you I will give the job all I got. I'll put my heart and soul into it. I'll work long hours. I'll study the problems the city can help with. I'll go out in the field and talk to people. Thank you from the bottom of my heart, Mr. Ibarra. I never expected something so wonderful."

Tears welled in David's eyes but didn't run down his cheeks.

Paul rose, walked over to Mr. Ibarra, and took his hand. "Even when we didn't see eye to eye, Mr. Ibarra," he told the man, "I never disrespected you. I knew you were one of the good guys. But now I know you're one of the great ones."

Carmen flew into her father's arms, squealing with delight. "I love you, Papa. Love you! Love you!" she cried.

Later, Paul and David were driving home. Paul gasped, "Man, I'm still in shock. I never saw that coming. I never had a clue."

"Paul," David responded, "it's something I never dreamed could happen for me again. I took a couple classes in prison in public relations, along with accounting. But I never thought I'd get something like this. You know, I'm gonna work harder than I've ever worked before. I'm gonna nail that job. I want Mr. Ibarra to be glad he did this for me. I won't let him down."

"A staff job in a councilman's office," Paul said, shaking his head. "No wonder Carmen is such a beautiful soul. For her old man to go pull something like this for a guy who needs a hand up, I'm like in awe. I'm kind of a cynic, you know, but this rocks me back on my heels. The goodness of humanity. Hah! Maybe it ain't just a myth."

David's cell phone rang then. "Yeah?" he said. "Oh, okay. Fine. Thanks for callin'." David ended he call, then broke out laughing. "It was the yogurt shop, bro. They didn't want me!" For most of the ride, they stopped laughing only to catch their breath.

By the next Monday morning, David Morales had filled out all the employment paperwork and had been oriented at the councilman's office. Also, with a loan from Paul, he bought some business clothes. Now David put on a blue striped shirt, a tie, blue dress pants, and new shoes. Paul drove him to the downtown office of Emilio Zapata Ibarra. The two young men high-fived each other. Paul drove on to work as David took the elevator up.

When David reported to Mr. Ibarra, the councilman was in his shirt sleeves, sitting at his desk. "Good morning, David," he said. "Listen, there's already a nut sitting out there waiting to talk to me. He's been here since eight o'clock so . . ."

David nodded. "I'll go talk to him right away, Mr. Ibarra."

David had a small cubicle down the hall. In it were a desk and a chair for a visitor.

He smiled at the man waiting outside the office. "Sir," he told the man, "I'm one of Councilman Ibarra's staff. I'll be glad to help you with your problem. Would you like to sit down with me and tell me what you need?"

"I want to talk to *somebody*," the man growled. "I've been given the runaround for two weeks, and I'm fuming. We got a big problem on our street, and that stiff in there don't care. I know how that guy works. He don't do nothin' unless you hold his feet to the fire. He's in there." The man bobbed his head toward the councilman's door. "I know he is. He's just duckin' me."

"Let's step down the hallway, sir," David suggested. "We'll see what we can do."

Seated in the cubicle, David asked, "So what would you like to talk about?"

"I live over there on Bluebird Street," the man began. "Ain't no rich folks living there. That's the problem—just ordinary folks struggling to survive. Old Ibarra, he's been ignoring everybody who ain't got deep pockets. I ain't surprised. I knew he was a bum when he got elected."

The man seemed to take a closer look at David. "You know, you're a young fella, ain't been around long. But let me tell you, used to be a councilman in this district, a prince of a man, Monte Esposito. He got stuff done for people. But this clown Ibarra, he took the job away from him in some underhanded way."

David seriously disagreed with what the man was saying, but he didn't let his feelings show. "Well," he responded, "let's hear about your problem, sir. I don't believe I got your name."

"Felix Martinez," he announced.

The name "Martinez" rang a bell. He wondered whether this man could be related to Ernesto's girlfriend, Naomi. David extended his hand. "Good to meet you, Mr. Martinez. I'm David. Just started on the staff here."

"Street lights, that's the problem, David," Mr. Martinez declared. "They got shot out by some lousy punks. Now it's so dark that the criminals got a field day. Poor old ladies comin' down the street are afraid of gettin' mugged. People don' go out at night no more. No offense, David, but you're obviously a clean-cut preppy kid who ain't got a clue about that side of life."

David almost chuckled at that remark. "But it's a zoo out there," Mr. Martinez went on. "Them wild animals are on the prowl in the dark. I got a beautiful seventeen-year-old girl, and I'm scared for her. My poor wife, she's a wimp, and she's afraid to go out at night at all. But the gangbangers do fine in the dark. They're on the prowl. They call it duck hunting. So we gotta get those lights fixed, David."

David took out a special pad for citizen complaints. As he jotted down information, Mr. Martinez sneered. "I know what's goin' down here. You write stuff on your little paper—my name, address. Then you file the paper, and nothin' gets done. I been down this road before."

"No, sir," David objected. "I agree with you. You have a serious problem over there. I understand where you're coming from. I'm grateful you came in here today and talked about it. So many people notice things wrong and just shrug them off. You did something. I'm putting in a work order for street light maintenance on this right away. This is a public safety issue, and you are going to see action. I promise."

David wasn't making it up. From his orientation, he knew how much he could do on his own and how much he needed to refer to Councilman Ibarra.

Felix Martinez smiled a little. "You're all right, kid. The gal they had in here before, she wouldn't give me the time of day. She had the nerve to tell me I was a pest and I should get a life. She told me that right to my face. I guess old Ibarra fired her and hired you. First good move that blowhard ever made."

Felix Martinez was leaving the cubicle when he turned and asked, "What's your full name, David?"

"Uh . . . ," David muttered, "Morales. David Morales."

Mr. Martinez's eyes widened. "No relation to Paul Morales, are you?" he asked.

"Yes, he's my brother," David replied, hoping the man had no beef with Paul.

"Great kid," Felix Martinez declared. "He hangs out with my girl Naomi and her boyfriend."

"Again, thank you for coming in, Mr. Martinez, and I'll see your street light problem is taken care of quickly," David assured him.

The moment Felix Martinez was out the door, Mr. Ibarra's office door opened. The councilman peered out.

"This was your baptism by fire, David," Mr. Ibarra remarked. "I heard the exchange, and I am impressed. Felix Martinez and I are . . . uh . . . on speaking terms. But the less speaking we do, the better I like it."

David smiled. "He's an okay guy. I'm getting street light maintenance on this right away. I'm putting a rush on the order. I don't blame those people on Bluebird Street for being scared of the dark. A lotta guys in prison told me their work was a whole lot easier when the street lights were out. All kinds of crime went up."

Emilio Ibarra grinned. "You know, David," he commented, "everything happens for a reason. You learned how to handle difficult people the hard way, but that's a skill. That's a real valuable skill. Good for you, *muchacho*."

David looked at the man with a fresh surge of gratitude. "Thanks again, Mr. Ibarra," he responded, "for giving me this chance. I'll never forget it. Never. But you know, Mr. Ibarra," David went on, "calling maintenance in is only a fix. It's not a solution."

"What do you mean?" the councilman asked.

"Well," David explained, "the creeps still have guns. They'll start taking target practice on those lights in days. We need a long-term solution. Don't know what it'd be. Maybe more cops, maybe some kind of bulletproof cover. Don't know. But we should be thinking about that."

Councilman Ibarra smiled broadly. "Have my assistant put it on the agenda for the council meeting today. We'll see what we can do. Maybe someone will have a bright idea."

Mr. Ibarra had three staff members, including David. Jeff Caudillo was a serious twenty-five-year-old man who had worked on Mr. Ibarra's campaign. The third staff member was Livy Majors, a pretty blonde just out of college. She wasn't working today, but Jeff came in soon after Mr. Martinez left. Emilio Ibarra had told David privately that he hadn't told the other staff members about David's past. Mr. Ibarra told David it was up to him how much, if anything, he wanted to share about his personal life.

Mr. Ibarra introduced David Morales to Jeff Caudillo. Then they worked at their desks, taking turns dealing with citizen complaints.

By two in the afternoon, it was David's turn. A very distraught woman in her late thirties demanded to see Councilman Ibarra. She kept saying how hard she had worked on Mr. Ibarra's election, and now he had to help her.

David asked the woman to wait a moment. He went into Mr. Ibarra's office, closing the door behind him. "Mr. Ibarra, there's a lady out there, Clare Padilla," he said. "She's pleading to see you personally."

Emilio Ibarra clamped his hands to his head. "David, I have a council meeting in five minutes. I haven't time to talk to her again. I've talked to her before. Her son is missing. The boy is fourteen. This is a matter for the police. He ran away from home after an argument with his mother. What can I do?"

David took a deep breath and went back into the outer office. Mrs. Padilla was waiting anxiously. She was shaking and wiping the tears from her eyes.

"Mrs. Padilla, Councilman Ibarra must go to a council meeting right now," David explained.

"*Mi niño*," the woman sobbed. "He's just a baby! He has been gone a week now. The police cannot find him. They say runaways come home eventually, but I am heartbroken. Councilman Ibarra promised if he was elected he would be like a father to us. Now he is too busy to help a mother. I will sit right here and wait for him to come back from his meeting."

Jeff Caudillo came out of his cubicle. "Ma'am, these council meetings sometimes go into the night."

"I don't care," Clare Padilla cried. "I will wait." She sat stock still, staring at the wall across the hallway.

Jeff looked at David and shook his head. Then he turned to the woman.

"We're closing this office early today, ma'am, because of the council meeting. Unless you leave, we'll have to call security. You could be arrested for trespassing. I'm sorry about your son, but it's not a matter for the city council. I'm sure the police are doing all they can to find the boy."

Tears streamed down the woman's face. "He is my only child," the woman sniffed, not looking at either of the young men. "My husband has gone from us. I have no parents. All I have in the world is Bobby. Have me arrested if you want. I have nothing to live for anyway."

Jeff looked at David again and said, "I'll get security."

"No, wait," David ordered. "Just give me five minutes with her."

Jeff shrugged his shoulders and returned to his computer.

David sat in a chair near the woman. "Do you have a photograph of your son, Mrs. Padilla?"

A glimmer of hope came into the woman's red-rimmed eyes. "Yes, yes," she cried, groping in her purse and digging out a school picture. "He is in the ninth grade at Cesar Chavez High School. He's a good boy. He has never been in bad trouble. It is my fault what happened. He stayed late at school to play basketball with his friends. I scolded him, and he yelled at me. I threatened to send him to his father. Then he ran away."

"Let me have the picture, Mrs. Padilla," David asked. "I'll make sure my friends at Chavez know the boy is missing. They'll be on the lookout for him. Maybe some of the students there can help us. Give me your home address and your phone number. A couple friends are very hooked up with what goes on in the *barrio*. I promise you, we'll do all we can to find your boy, Mrs. Padilla."

The woman calmed down. "*Gracias*," she murmured. "I am so scared for Bobby. He is out there alone in this bad world, and he is so young. I do the best I can, but I am only a cleaning lady. I can't give Bobby nice things like the other children have."

"Listen," David told the woman gently. "Here's my cell phone number. If your son comes home, call me. My name is David Morales. I'll make copies of this picture of Bobby and give them to my friends. I think we'll find him."

"*Gracias a Dios*," Mrs. Padilla sighed. "*Gracias a Dios*." She stood up, walked slowly to the door, and left.

Jeff had had stepped out of the office. Now, as he returned, he saw Mrs. Padilla leaving. "Oh, did you finally convince her that we were serious about getting security up here?"

"No," David replied.

"How did you get rid of her then?" Jeff asked.

David walked over to the copying machine and started making twenty copies of Bobby Padilla's picture. "I told her we'd try to help her find her son," David responded.

"Morales, listen," Jeff Caudillo scolded in an annoyed voice. "That's not what we're about around here. We fix potholes and straighten out zoning problems and get the city budget put together."

"I think Mr. Ibarra wants us to help the people in the *barrio* any way we can," David insisted. "I get what you're sayin', Jeff, and you're right. I'll put in my time as a staff member here. But I'm pretty sure some of my friends can help me find this kid. I'll do it on my personal time. I'm just gonna ask my friends to keep an eye out for the kid. Maybe we can do the poor woman some good."

Jeff Caudillo sat down at his desk and laughed. "Another bleeding heart liberal. Hey, David, good luck to you. I don't know where you come from. But here in the real world there are very few happy endings. But give it a shot. I think the councilman'd be very happy with what you've done, but I sure wouldn't have done it."

# CHAPTER SIX

A little later, Paul Morales pulled into the parking lot of the city council building. David jumped into the cab.

"How'd it go, man?" Paul asked. "I was shaky all day. I wanted to call you, but I didn't wanna spook the deal."

"Dude," David exclaimed, "it was the best day of my life! I felt at home there. I was helpin' people. I can't tell you what this means to me. I've spent hours and hours studying the city agencies. I know what I'm talking about when people call. It's great. Only one thing . . ."

"Uh-oh," Paul reacted.

"No, see," David explained, "this lady came in. She was all hysterical because her fourteen-year-old boy ran away. Been gone a week. She was bound and determined that Councilman Ibarra could help her. But he had to get to a council meeting."

"The cops are supposed to look for lost kids," Paul said.

"Yeah, I know," David admitted. "But she said the police just told her he was a runaway, and he'd come home soon on his own. The poor lady, she was outta her mind. She gave me a picture of the boy, and I made twenty copies. You know so many guys, Paul, like Cruz and Beto. They seem to know what's going down all over the *barrio*. I was thinking maybe if you . . ."

Paul looked over at his brother and grinned. "*Hermano*, of course I'll help. I'll get all my low-down friends to keep an eye out for the little *muchacho*. We'll pass out the pictures. My homies'll turn over some rocks."

"Thanks, Paul," David said, leaning back in the seat against the headrest and closing his eyes. "Man, I never thought I could have a day like this in my life. Lying on that cot in prison, I thought life would never be good again. I thought I'd be lucky to be washing cars or waiting tables for the rest of my life. I never dreamed somebody would give me a chance at a job like this."

David shook his head, as if trying to get a bad memory out of his mind. "When Hawthorne gave me that ear bangin', I felt whupped. I felt like I didn't have a chance."

Paul never took his eyes off the road. He just spoke flatly. "Unbroken, man."

"Yep," David responded. "Unbroken."

Paul smiled and winked at his brother.

"Hey," Paul said after a moment, "Naomi texted me that her father was down at Councilman Ibarra's office. He wanted to get the streetlights fixed on Bluebird. You didn't run into Felix Martinez by any chance, did you?"

"Yeah, he was my first customer!" David chuckled. "Really gave me an earful about what a crummy guy poor Mr. Ibarra is. But I got along fine with him. I put in a rush order to the street light maintenance people to get the lights fixed. I told them it was a safety problem and the police want the lights fixed in a hurry. Boy, that got their attention."

"Dude," Paul remarked, "you're gonna be the star in this family pretty soon."

"In my book, you're *always* gonna be the star," David responded. Then, in a softer voice, he asked, "Paul, do you believe in heaven?"

"I guess so," Paul replied. "Gotta be something better than this down the road. Or else, what are we doing here?"

"Our mom, she believed in heaven, you know," David told his brother. "She was so strung out on drugs by the time you got to know her . . . Well, she started goin' downhill fast when you were about six. But I knew her when she still had some good days."

David stared straight ahead through the windshield. He was remembering a good time in his life. "I was nine—almost nine—and we went to an amusement park. She said if anything ever happened to her, I shouldn't be sad. She'll be lookin' after me from heaven. I didn't want to hear about anything happening to her. She was our mom. She was all we had. But now I think sometimes she *was* helpin' me when I was in prison. Maybe she put the idea of hirin' me into Mr. Ibarra's head. You think, Paul?"

"She'd do it if she could, that's for sure," Paul agreed. "Moms are like that, even lousy moms. I'll tell you one thing, dude. I never in a million years expected Mr. Ibarra would do something like that. He's a good man, but that was a big stretch. It almost hadda be some kinda miracle."

David smiled. "I think so too." He took one of the pictures of Bobby Padilla from his wallet and looked at it. Maybe there was a miracle out there for Bobby too.

Just about then, they reached their apartment lot. David looked up from the photo and cried, "What's that *thing* in our parking lot?"

"My new wheels, man. You can have your truck back. I'm now a Jagman," Paul announced, laughing.

"You bought a Jaguar?" David gasped, staring at the beautiful electric blue car. "Man, did you win the lottery?"

Paul laughed harder. "Nah, it's an old Jag, but in great shape. Nice old lady always comes in the electronics shop. She knows from nothing about the new gadgets. So I take the time to explain stuff to her—how to connect her answering machine to the phone, the glitches on her computer. She's stuck in the eighteen hundreds."

Paul parked the truck and handed the key to David. They got out of the cab and walked toward the Jaguar. "Anyway," Paul continued, "her husband died a while back. It was his Jag. He loved the car, treated it like a baby. The Jag's older than me, and she let me have it crazy cheap. She told me I been so nice to her that Marvin—that's her husband—would want me to have it. I'm telling you this, David, but you gotta swear not to tell anybody else. It'd ruin my whole image if people knew. But some little-blue haired lady has adopted me as her grandson!"

They stood in front of the Jaguar. "It's awesome, eh?" Paul remarked.

"Yeah!" David responded. They circled the car once or twice, commenting on this or that. "It's bad, Paul," David commented.

Then David remembered the pictures of Bobby Padilla in his wallet. "Could you get a couple of these to Ernesto?"

"Sure, me and Carmen are hanging out with him and Naomi tonight," Paul replied. "Now there's a dude, that Ernie. That old lady should really be adopting him. He's really the nice guy."

"So are you, man," David insisted. "But it's our secret."

Ernesto Sandoval had a senior class meeting the next afternoon. As senior class president, he presided over the meetings at Cesar Chavez High. The meetings usually went well except for static he got from a couple of the seniors. One was Rod Garcia, who he beat out for senior class president in the election. The other was Clay Aguirre, who had hated Ernesto for a long time. Rod would never get over losing the election to Ernesto. And Clay would never forgive Ernesto for taking Naomi Martinez away from him.

"We got some important things on the agenda today," Ernesto announced to a packed auditorium.

The senior class was very involved this year. Ernesto had gotten them helping with several projects. Ernesto had a lot of enthusiasm, and it rubbed off on most of the other seniors.

"We're running that Saturday car wash," he stated, "to raise money to send ten students to the model United Nations. And we got to plan Grandparents Day. That's gonna be a big thing. It wasn't well attended last year, but this year's gonna be different. Ms. Wilson's reminded me how many grandparents are involved with the students here. Sometimes they're the only parents." Deprise Wilson was the bubbly senior class faculty advisor.

Then Ernesto said, "Before we get to anything else, I have a kind of unusual request. A freshman boy here at Chavez has gone missing. I know some of you guys are already into planning for a program where we help struggling freshman. But this is an emergency. He's been missing for a week, and his mom's a single parent. She's out of her mind with worry. The police have him down as a missing person, but they haven't found him. He's just another runaway. A friend of mine is on the staff of Councilman Emilio Ibarra. This request comes from there."

Ernesto held up a handful of paper as he spoke. "I've printed out enough pictures of Bobby Padilla so you all will have a copy. On the back of the picture are the phone numbers of Mrs. Padilla and my friend in Mr. Ibarra's office. If we all keep our eyes open, we might be able to do something really great. We could find this kid before something happens to him."

As they were passing out the pictures, Rod Garcia raised his hand. "Ernie, I think this is ridiculous. We're wasting valuable time at our senior class meeting to try and find someone. And who is it but a little gangbanger punk who ran away from home? Actually, this isn't the first time you've had a personal agenda during these meetings. I don't think I'm the only one who's sick of it."

"Yeah!" a girl responded. She'd been buffing her fingernails during Ernesto's presentation, but now she came alive. "Our meetings should be about us."

Ernesto struggled to keep his usual composure. "Thanks for your input. I'm always glad to hear other opinions. We're not gonna spend a lotta time on this. We have many other things to deal with. But I don't think most of you mind spending four minutes on it. Just take a picture and keep your eyes open over the next few days. It's voluntary."

Abel Ruiz and Naomi Martinez quickly passed out the pictures of Bobby Padilla.

Rod Garcia continued trying to make Ernesto look bad. "You're kind of a megalomaniac, Ernie. You're so full of your own sense of importance that you think you can save the world. You're willing to sacrifice the time and energy of the whole senior class for your own purposes. We need to make this a great senior year for us, and it's not happening, man."

Deprise Wilson raised her hand and Ernesto recognized her. "The teachers who've been here for a long time—maybe ten and fifteen years—are saying wonderful things about this class. They're telling me they have never seen such a spirited, enthusiastic, compassionate senior class. I see it myself. Kids are caring about each other, even about strangers, in a way I've never seen. You guys want a great senior year? You're well on the way."

Wild applause broke out all over the auditorium, and Rod Garcia looked very dejected.

After school, Ernesto called David Morales. He told David that he'd made copies of Bobby Padilla's picture for all the seniors. He mentioned that he'd put David's cell phone number on the back of the copies. "That's gonna be a lot of coverage, David," Ernesto said.

"You're awesome, dude," David responded. "Paul told me you were the most good-hearted person he ever met, and it's true."

"David, there are a lotta kids at Chavez with big hearts," Ernesto declared. "A few of the other kind, but we won't think about that right now."

"I hear you, man," David replied. "I just got off the phone with a psycho. He swore that he read an article in the paper. Councilman Ibarra, he says, just voted to double his own salary and cut the pay of police officers and firefighters. It never happened, man. But this guy was yelling and cussing and asking me if council members could be impeached. Some people aren't happy unless they're making other people miserable."

"Know what, though, David?" Ernesto remarked. "Last night, when I went to visit Naomi, the street lights were burning bright on Bluebird Street."

"*Ay! Gracias a Dios!*" David exclaimed. "They promised me at street light maintenance they'd get on it fast, and they did!"

A little later that day, David was working on his computer, checking with the road department about some serious potholes. Mr. Ibarra came out of his office and spoke to David, Jeff, and Livy. "We have the one cent sales tax increase on the council agenda today. Nobody likes to raise taxes, but we've already made painful cuts in every department. It's either the tax or brownouts at the fire stations. That could mean closing down some stations. And that could be the difference between life and death for somebody—some little kid choking or a heart attack victim."

The councilman's brow became wrinkled. "But tonight on the local news, they're going to be calling us 'the tax and spend crowd' again. I've already heard lies on the Internet. And the radio shock jocks will be working the public into a frenzy. You guys have to get ready for the irate taxpayer calls. Calm and nice is the word, even if they're cursing us all out."

"I take it you're gonna vote for the one cent increase, huh, Mr. Ibarra?" Jeff asked.

"Of course," Emilio Zapata Ibarra boomed, his mustache dancing over his lips. "What can we do? We've already cut the library hours. We've cut staff in all the departments. The federal government can just print more money or borrow from China, but cities can't do that. We've got to have money to put gas in the fire engines and the patrol cars!" Mr. Ibarra was red in the face as he stomped into his office.

Livy Majors was at the desk next to David. She looked fragile, but she was tough. She had a black belt in karate. In the short time David had worked here, he'd seen her deal masterfully with angry citizens. "I'm going to be finished with college next semester, but I'm going to continue working here. I like the political circus. If all the good, dedicated people abandon ship, we're all sunk. We've got the best government in the world in this country, and we need to make it work."

David looked at the young woman with admiration. He wished more than ever that he wasn't an ex-convict. If he were just a young man finishing his own college degree, he might ask Livy to join him for a cup of coffee. But doing that was totally out of the question; it struck him as insane.

David winced at the thought of either Jeff or Livy learning of his true background. Anyway, he thought, this lovely, professional girl had to have a fine boyfriend of quality. David felt a little sick to his stomach to imagine the look on Livy's face if she were to find out where he'd been for the past two years. David himself shuddered to recall the company he had kept in those cell blocks. He'd seen the terrible ugliness of men stripped of all dignity, reduced to brutes.

The phone rang on David's desk.

"I wanna express my opposition to the fifty cent sales tax increase," a woman said in a high-pitched voice. "Do you realize what that will mean to everything we buy? We're middle class people and—"

"Excuse me, ma'am," David broke in. "It's a one cent sales tax increase. One cent added to the present rate."

"I don't believe that," the woman declared. "The man on the radio said it was fifty cents."

"Yes, ma'am, I'm sure that's what you heard," David responded. "But the man made a mistake."

"Well, I don't want those crooks down there raising my taxes," the woman raved on. "I work hard, and I can't afford more taxes. Councilman Ibarra is just like all the rest. They're livin' large, and they want us poor workin' people to pay for it all."

"Well, ma'am," David replied, "I will certainly share your opinions with the councilman. Thank you so much for calling."

The next caller had a different complaint. "Those blasted dogs are tearin' up my rose garden again." David had no idea who those "blasted dogs" were. "Isn't there a law against dogs runnin' loose without a leash? They're runnin' around, destroyin' other people's property. I'm a senior citizen, and I fought in two wars. And I think I have the right to enjoy my rose garden without my neighbor's Rottweilers running through it."

"Yes, sir, you're right," David answered. He was relieved that the solution was simple. "There is a law against unleashed dogs. When dogs are not on their own property, they have to be leashed. You need to call Animal Control. They'll send someone out to speak with the owner. I'll give you their number."

CHAPTER SIX

"Could you tell Councilman Ibarra that I voted for him?" the man asked. "I'd appreciate it if he would take a hand in this. He might even remember me at one of his rallies. I'm six foot six, and he commented about how tall I was."

"Yes, sir, I'll tell him," David replied. "I'm sure Councilman Ibarra appreciates your support. And thank you for serving our country. However, we just don't have people down here in the City Council to deal with dogs on the loose. So if you would call Animal Control—"

"Passin' the buck," the man snarled. "That's what I call it. Just passin' the buck. Well, thanks for nothing."

"Well, hold on a second, sir," David said, just before the man was about to hang up. "Why don't you give me your name, address, and phone number. We'll make the call for you. Maybe we'll get a little faster action for you."

"Well, that's more like it," the man responded, a little less angrily. David spent a few minutes on the line taking down the information.

When David hung up, Jeff glanced over at him, a smirk on his face. "You mean you're not personally going out with a net to round up the dogs, David?"

David laughed and made the quick call to Animal Control. Then Jeff spoke to David.

"Last week I got a call from a guy saying that the councilman was doing a good job," Jeff remarked. "I almost fell off my chair. You get so few of those."

"Mr. Ibarra *is* doing a great job," Livy remarked. "Just one thing alone has impressed me so much. You know that Nicolo Sena Scholarship program from years ago? Business and government sponsored promising kids for college. It was named for the first Hispanic boy from the *barrio* who died in Vietnam."

David had heard about it. "Well," Livy went on, "when Monte Esposito was councilman, he didn't go out and enlist businesses, so the scholarship went unfunded and died out. Mr. Ibarra got it going again. He almost went on his knees to local businesses, pleading for matching funds. Not many people know this. But he put some of his own money in, and he's not a rich man. Now kids who couldn't have afforded college can go. I feel so proud to be working for a man like that."

"Yep," David agreed, "he's a pretty wonderful guy."

Livy Majors looked at David and smiled. It was a very warm smile. If things were different, David might have gotten ideas about dating her.

"You know," David commented to Livy Majors, "I have a friend, Ernie Sandoval. His father got his teacher training through that scholarship. Ernie's uncle, he's a lawyer. He got help from the scholarship too."

"Yeah," Livy said. "My mother got her nursing school education that way too. Before the Nicolo Sena fund, there was nothing in the *barrio* that targeted poor Hispanic kids. It was always my mom's dream to be a nurse, and that made it possible. Now she's an RN in intensive care at the hospital, and she's so happy."

Livy noted David's puzzlement and smiled. David's expression said, "But you're not Hispanic."

Livy explained. "My mom's maiden name is Bejarano."

"Oh, I see," David said, returning her smile.

# CHAPTER SEVEN

David went on to solve several small problems over the rest of the afternoon. At the end of his day, he went down to the pickup truck for the trip home. For the first time in more than two years, he unlocked his own vehicle. "Hey," he thought, "I'm gonna do the afternoon rush hour like a normal person."

He'd bought the pickup shortly before he was arrested. Paul had just started to drive at the time, and David often loaned the truck to his kid brother. When David was sent to prison, the truck became Paul's wheels. Now that Paul had the Jaguar, David had his wheels back.

David had missed so many of the ordinary things in prison. Stopping by a fast-food place to grab something he was suddenly hungry for . . . buying a new pair of jeans at the big box store . . . just taking off for the beach when he felt like cooling off. Perhaps most of all, he missed sticking his key into the ignition and driving. That was something he missed every day. And now, as David merged into the flow of traffic, he felt exhilarated. He was just another young dude coming home from work.

David was pulling into the apartment parking lot when his phone rang. He parked and grabbed his cell. "Yeah?"

"David," Emilio Ibarra said, "the council meeting just ended. We passed the one cent sales tax increase, thank God. We won't have to lay off any more cops."

"That's great, Mr. Ibarra," David responded. "I guess we'll get some calls tomorrow."

"You can bet on it," the councilman replied. "Listen, David, I tried to get you before you left today, so I'll tell you now. This won't wait until tomorrow."

David froze in apprehension. Things were going too well. Something bad had to happen. Maybe somebody found out about his past. Maybe someone important resented his being on Mr. Ibarra's staff. David broke out in a cold sweat. "Yeah," he said, "what's up?"

"David," Mr. Ibarra answered, "I am hearing so many good things about you. There is one guy, I could have sworn he was the devil. He's been a thorn in my side since I got this job. He texted me earlier today. He said a young guy in my office— David-something—finally treated him like a human being. He said you didn't even laugh at him. You know the one I mean, David. He'd been abducted by aliens who planted a radio receiver in his brain."

"Oh yeah," David recalled. He smiled, relieved that he wasn't in trouble. "The guy with the aluminum foil turban. How could I forget him? He's so lonely; all he does is watch those shows about aliens. But he's not a bad dude. He actually gave me ten bucks for the Sena Scholarship fund. Thanks for telling me, Mr. Ibarra."

"Thank *you*," Mr. Ibarra responded, "for being much more than I thought when I hired you, David."

The councilman had to end the call then.

As David put the phone in his pocket, he said softly, "No, sir, *thank you*." As David walked to the apartment, he thought about the elderly man who said he was abducted. He remembered the desperate look in the man's eyes. The old man had mental problems, but he was harmless. All David did for him was to treat him with respect. In the end, it was all the man wanted. David told the man that the aliens probably meant no harm. But if anything really bad happened, he should call David's direct line at the office. David would talk to him again.

On his way to Cesar Chavez High the next morning. Ernesto Sandoval was thinking about Grandparents Day. He had to get the committee on that project started. He was delighted that so many kids were getting involved. They'd prepare a nice breakfast. Then they'd put on a fashion show and music revue. It would feature the songs their grandparents would remember from years ago. Finally, of course, there'd be the cleanup.

As Ernesto walked from the parking lot, he noticed Clay Aguirre walking toward him. Ernesto sighed inwardly. "This can't be good," he thought. So early in the morning and already a problem.

"Hey, Sandoval," Clay cried, "you know that stupid kid's picture you passed out at the senior meeting?"

"Yes," Ernesto sighed, "I'm sorry if it bothered you, Clay. Rod Garcia already made it clear that it bothered some people. He didn't want to take time from senior class business to find a lost kid. Actually—"

Clay cut him off. "On the back of the picture, there's somebody's cell number—a dude named David. I don't know this jerk, and I don't want to get mixed up with him. The thing is, I mighta seen the kid."

Ernesto looked at Clay with shock. "Oh man, really? Where?"

"Don't get all excited," Clay demanded. "And don't tell anybody I came to you about this. I don't want them thinking . . ." His voice trailed. "Anyway, I was over on Polk this morning, down by the old empty warehouses. I needed to pick up some salmon for my parents. There's a fish market down there."

Ernesto's look probably was saying, "C'mon, man, get to the point."

"Anyway," Clay went on, "I seen this kid going through a dumpster. It was right next to a little Asian market. I guess the market tosses leftover food. The kid was in the dumpster, looking for food, I guess. I can't swear it was him, but it looked like the kid in the picture."

"Oh man, thanks, Clay!" Ernesto exclaimed. "I know you don't like me. But you were man enough to put that aside for the sake of the kid. I give you props for that, dude."

"Ah, skip the mush, Sandoval," Clay replied sourly. "Probably isn't even the kid you're looking for." Clay turned and hurried away, as if he were embarrassed by his own act of decency.

Ernesto got on his cell phone and called David Morales. He told him what Clay had said. "We're not sure, of course, but . . ."

"Thanks, Ernie," David said. He jumped up from his desk and went into Mr. Ibarra's office. "Mr. Ibarra, do you remember that lady, Mrs. Padilla?"

Mr. Ibarra clasped his head. "Don't tell me she's here again!" he groaned.

"No, listen," David responded excitedly. "Some friends of mine passed her kid's picture around, and they maybe got a lead. He may be hiding in an old warehouse on Polk. The guy saw him climbing in a dumpster and looking for food."

Mr. Ibarra's face dissolved in horror. "*Ay, Dios mio!*"

"Mr. Ibarra, I know this is asking a lot," David inquired. "But could I have a little time off to go down there and see if it's Bobby? Who knows what could happen to a little guy like that."

"Of course, yes, yes," Mr. Ibarra agreed. "The day is thankfully quiet. Jeff and I can handle the office." He rose and led the way to Livy's desk. To her, the councilman said, "David thinks they may have spotted Mrs. Padilla's lost boy. I think it would be good if you went with David. The boy must be terrified, and if he sees a girl . . ."

"Yes, certainly," Livy Majors replied, grabbing her sweater against the chill wind outside.

They went to David's pickup. As the truck pulled out of the lot, Livy posed a question. "What's the story about the boy? I never dealt with his mother."

"He had a fight with his mother," David explained. "And she threatened to send him to his father. The parents are divorced, and the boy's frightened of his father. Bobby

130

Padilla's been away from home for a week, and he's only fourteen years old. His mother's devastated. She said the boy is all she has in the world. She says she wouldn't want to live if . . . you know, something happened to him."

"Poor woman!" Livy gasped. "But why did she keep coming to Mr. Ibarra's office for help? Why didn't she call the police?"

"She did call the police," David answered. "But there are just too many runaways. The police do their best, but I guess there're thousands of such kids. If the police think the kid's been kidnapped, then they go all out but . . . Anyway, she said she voted for Mr. Ibarra, and she thought he might be able to help. Then I got into it."

"Oh, David," Livy commented, "you really put your heart into your job. You're such a good heart." She reached over and patted David's knee. "You must have wonderful parents to have raised such a compassionate person."

David didn't say anything as they turned onto the freeway ramp. But the moment the girl had touched his knee, he trembled inside. He realized again that he had feelings for a girl.

"We seem about the same age, David," Livy remarked. "I graduated from Cesar Chavez High about five years ago, but I don't remember you. Of course, it's a big school."

"Uh, I didn't go to Chavez," David explained. "I was living in Los Angeles at the time. We moved down here, my brother and me, and he went to Chavez. He's younger than me."

"Oh!" Livy responded. "Well, if he's younger than you, then I wouldn't have known him either."

David was glad for the Washington turnoff. They were almost there. David remembered the old warehouse and the Asian market on Polk. It had been started decades ago by refugees from Vietnam who were called the "boat people."

David drove slowly down Polk Street, looking for the Asian market. "Look," Livy pointed, "that brick building with all the signs in Vietnamese."

"Yeah, and the warehouse," David noted. "It's got broken windows. Easy for a kid to get in. It's awful to think of a four-teen-year-old kid in there with maybe dangerous older men. He's gotta be scared, but what's he gonna do? He hates his father, and he thinks his mother doesn't love him anymore. He has nowhere to go."

"David, the way you talk about it," Livy commented, "it almost sounds as if something similar happened to you. Did you ever run away from home?" Livy's eyes filled with interest.

"Uh yeah, a few times," David admitted. But he hadn't really run away from home. He'd run away from the dysfunctional families he was placed with. By the time David was fourteen, home was a distant memory.

They parked and got out of the truck, walking slowly toward the warehouse.

"Livy, there may be a back entrance," David said. "When he hears somebody coming in the front, he might just try to run out the back. I'm goin' around the back. You go in that door that's ajar, but be real careful. Open it slowly, and call his name—Bobby. If he hears a female voice, it could put him at ease a little."

Livy Majors waited a few seconds for David to get around to the back. Then she gently pushed the front door open and called out. "Bobby? It's okay, Bobby. We came to help you. Don't be afraid."

A wild clatter erupted inside. Someone had been sitting on a crate, eating whatever he found in the dumpster. He flew toward the back door. As he exploded out into the alley, David grabbed him.

"It's okay, *muchacho*," David assured him. "Nobody's gonna hurt you. Take it easy."

The boy struggled against David, kicking him violently in his shins. Terror filled the boy's dark eyes as David held his thin shoulders firmly.

The boy was Bobby Padilla all right. There was no mistaking those big brown eyes, the small cleft in his chin.

Livy Majors arrived around to the back quickly, having heard the commotion. The sight of her seemed to quiet the boy a little. "Bobby," Livy said softly. "We're here to help you. You don't belong living in a dirty, cold warehouse."

"Lemme alone!" Bobby Padilla sobbed, big tears rolling down his brown cheeks. His hair was shining black, like a raven's wing.

David held firmly onto the boy's upper arm and guided him slowly to a grassy knoll behind the warehouse. "Bobby," David explained, "your mother's crying her eyes out. She wants you to come home. She's so sad without you that she doesn't want to live."

"No!" the boy cried defiantly. "She don't like me no more. She's gonna send me to *mi padre*, who beats me with a stick! She told me I'm bad, an' she don't want me no more."

"Bobby," David persisted, "she's sorry she said those mean things to you. She was worried about how you were acting. But she blames herself for being mean to you. She loves you, Bobby. She wants you to come home."

"I can't go home," the boy cried. "I *am* bad."

"Okay," David commanded, "calm down and stay right here a minute."

David dialed Mrs. Padilla's phone. When she heard David's voice, she asked excitedly, "You have news of my son?"

"Mrs. Padilla, Bobby's here with us. He's fine, but he's very scared and confused." David looked the boy up and down. "And pretty dirty too." To Bobby, he said teasingly, "Man, you gotta get home at least for a good hot shower." The boy's face seemed to relax a little.

"Bobby! *Mi hijo*!" Mrs. Padilla screamed so loudly that Bobby heard her voice. His eyes widened.

David handed the phone to Bobby. The boy was shaking and crying.

"Bobby," his mother sobbed, "I love you! I love you more than anything in the world. You are my heart and my soul. I am empty without *mi hijo*!"

"You said you'd send me to *mi padre*," the boy whispered.

"Never, never, *nunca*!" Mrs. Padilla pledged. "I swear I will never do that."

Bobby wiped his nose with his sleeve. His big brown eyes glistened with tears as he handed the phone back to David.

"Mrs. Padilla," David told the woman, "we're bringing him home."

They drove to the small apartment on Oriole Street. Mrs. Padilla was standing out in front. Then she saw the pickup truck with her son inside. Even before David brought it to a full stop, she ran toward the truck, screaming and crying. She grabbed Bobby as he climbed from the truck, kissing him and hugging him. She didn't care that he was very grimy and dirty from his week on the street. For the first time since David had seen Bobby, the boy laughed.

"No, Mama, no!" he begged, as she kissed him over and over. David could tell the boy was embarrassed, but he also looked happy.

Then Mrs. Padilla turned to David. Before he could stop her, she grabbed his hand and kissed it. Then she kissed Livy's hand. "You are *santos*," she cried. "I thought I would never see my little boy again, and you brought him home to me."

"I'm not a little boy, Mama," Bobby protested. "I'm almost a man."

"You are my baby!" Mrs. Padilla cried. She put her arm around the boy's shoulders and led him toward their apartment. Before going inside, Mrs. Padilla turned and waved to David and Livy. Bobby smiled a little and waved too. David could see that he was glad to be home. Bobby would not come right out and say it, but he had to be very glad to be home. The past week had to have been the most miserable of his life.

"Wow!" Livy exclaimed as she followed David back to his pickup. "This morning, all I was hoping for was a good hair day. Maybe a fresh BLT for lunch. Now I've been canonized! Think of it, David. We are *santos*!"

David laughed. "You were a big help, Livy. I couldn't have managed this without you. If I'd gone alone, the boy would have fled through the back door. We mighta lost him."

"Well, I'm glad I was helpful, David," Livy responded. "But the truth is, this is your project. You deserve the credit. What if I'd been in the office when Mrs. Padilla came in pleading for help in finding her son? I would have maybe called the police and asked them to look a little harder for Bobby. I wouldn't have got into it as you did. You're really incredibly special. I mean, Jeff's a great guy, efficient, hard working. But you . . . I mean, where do people like you come from?"

David wasn't going to answer that question. He held the door for Livy to get in the pickup.

When they got back to the office, the first person they saw was Jeff Caudillo. "Well," Jeff announced sarcastically, "here are the angels of mercy returning from their crusade. How did it go? Let's see. No puncture wounds. So the kid didn't try to stick you with a knife? He came peaceably?"

"He's just a scared little boy," David responded. "He was worried his mom was going to send him to his father—a kind of a brute, I guess. Once he knew we were on his side, it was fine."

David went into Mr. Ibarra's office to report. "I want to thank you for letting Livy and me look for Bobby. We found him and took him home."

"That's wonderful, David," Emilio Ibarra boomed with a big smile. "I got elected to this job so that I could help

140

people." The big man sighed. "And I try to do that. But most of the time I am caught in a web of taxes, fees, arguments in the council, irate citizens. When you do something like this from my office, David, you redeem me. You bring me to my core, for these are the things that really matter."

David thanked the councilman and left his office. Outside, he left a voice mail for Ernesto. "Dude, you passing out those pictures of Bobby was pure genius. We never would have found him otherwise. Thanks, Ernie."

Later, between classes, Ernesto got the message, smiled, and went looking for Clay Aguirre. "Hey, Aguirre," he shouted. "I gotta tell you something, man."

Clay turned. "Wasn't the kid, huh?" he asked. "I thought it probably wasn't, but it looked like him."

"It *was* the right kid," Ernesto answered. "David just texted me. They found the kid right where you said you saw him. They took him home to his mom. Thanks for the tip, man. Without it, the kid would still be out there. He'd be living in a dirty warehouse, maybe getting mugged or killed by some dopehead. You know what you did, Clay? You maybe saved the life of a four-teen-year-old boy."

Clay Aguirre looked shocked. "Yeah . . . well," he mumbled.

"Deal with it, man. You did something great," Ernesto insisted. "Would you accept a fist bump from an old enemy?"

Clay shrugged again, and the boys fist-bumped.

"I still don't like you, Sandoval," Clay grumbled.

"Same here, homie," Ernesto said, smiling and walking away.

# CHAPTER EIGHT

$W$hile David and Livy were out of the office, Jeff Caudillo had held the fort. Now, with them back, he went out for a late lunch. Emilio Ibarra was at a meeting trying to decide how to use the extra money from the added sales tax. The revenue had to be doled out to the police, the fire department, and all the other agencies.

From time to time as he worked the computer, David glanced at Livy. He didn't want to, but she had amazingly big gray eyes, flecked with silver and was very lovely. But he steeled himself against noticing that too much. Any relationship with her was totally out of the question. He struggled to keep a tight rein on his emotions.

Out of the blue, Livy commented, "I keep thinking about that poor little guy, Bobby. You wonder how these kids from troubled homes even survive. I mean, David, we're so lucky. We come from good families who always nurtured us. Like we took it for granted that Mom and Dad loved us and would do the right thing."

David ached to set her straight on his own background, but he kept quiet. Livy continued. "My own dad's a wonderful man. I was Daddy's little girl, and he couldn't do enough for me. Mom was the same way. Mom was always right there for me and my brother. Mom didn't even start her nursing career full time until we were both in school. Even then, she arranged her schedule so she'd be there every day. She'd welcome us home from school even if that meant working nights at the hospital. But kids like Bobby . . . His mother loves him, and she didn't mean to scare him off. But he's got a brutal father. What must that be like for a kid?"

David briefly closed his eyes. Terrible memories about foster care flooded back like a bloody tide. He shivered. Many children thrived with loving foster families. But David and Paul were not so lucky.

"You look so deep in thought, David," Livy commented. "Seeing somebody like Bobby makes us appreciate what we have, doesn't it?"

"Yeah," David replied. He was glad when the phone rang.

Near the end of the day, Jeff Caudillo suggested that they all meet at the coffee shop downstairs before going home. "They got great coffee and awesome scones down there," Jeff urged.

"I'm game," Livy agreed immediately. "It's been quite a day."

"Okay," David responded. But he still didn't feel comfortable with his fellow staff members.

Only a little later, they sat in the coffee shop, sipping coffee and waiting for their scones. Jeff remarked, "You know, Mr. Ibarra drives me crazy sometimes. But he's the most honest politician I've ever known, and I've worked with a few. I spent a year as an intern to a congressman in Washington, and, man, did my youthful idealism take a beating. The guy cheated on his wife and hit on the girl interns. He was so crooked that he joked about not being able to lie in bed straight. But Mr. Ibarra, he's so honest he won't even borrow paper clips to take home."

"Yes," Livy agreed, putting her coffee cup down. "Last month, some slick-looking guys came in trying to get a zone change. Someone wanted to put another bar on Polk Street, as if there aren't enough there already. *I know* they offered him money. He literally threw them out of his office. When the councilman pounds his fist on the desk, it's like an earthquake, and he sure did that day."

The scones were delivered to their table, and Livy beamed. "Oh, I *love* these. A little cream and sugar and golden brown. I've tried to make them at home, but they never come out this good."

David had never had a scone before. He didn't even know what it was, but he liked his. It went great with the coffee.

Jeff turned to David with a half smile on his face. "You're sort of an odd duck, David," Jeff commented. "I haven't figured you out yet, but I can tell you one thing. Mr. Ibarra really likes you. He's a good guy to work for, and he appreciates all his staff. But he's *really* high on you."

"Mr. Ibarra told me that too," Livy added, smiling. "He told me that when he hired you, David, he hit the jackpot."

"Thanks," David murmured. "I like working up there, and you guys are great to work with."

"Except when I'm trying to get security to throw some lady out of the office?" Jeff asked, teasingly. "You were right on that, David, but Mrs. Padilla made me nervous."

"You never know when somebody's going to get violent," Livy remarked, swallowing a bite of scone.

Finished with their scones and coffee, the three staff members headed home. In his truck on the freeway, David felt very good about how things were going. But he was still nervous. Nobody knew his background. Maybe if they did know, they would treat him differently. He knew his secret would eventually leak out. If they found out he was an ex-con, how would that change things? A lot of people could never forgive someone who'd been in prison.

When David got home, Paul was opening the box of hot pizza. "How'd it go, dude?" Paul asked.

"Good, real good," David answered. The pizza looked and smelled so good. Even though he wasn't hungry because of the scones, David decided to take a small slice.

"David, Carmen called me at work," Paul reported. "Her father told her what you did today. Dude, you rescued a poor kid from who knows what. I'm tellin' you, Carmen is about ready to put you in for canonization." Paul grinned. "I'm proud of you, *hermano*, really, really proud."

David stood there, pizza slice in hand, saying nothing. He couldn't remember Paul ever being that proud of him. Maybe he was once, ages ago when they were both kids. David had flown off the high ramp on his skateboard and landed erect. But he couldn't even remember that for sure.

"Thanks," David responded.

Paul leaned back on the sofa with his slice of pizza and asked, "Remember the Johnsons?"

"Yeah, the black family," David recalled. "I guess they were our foster parents when I was about thirteen and you were ten. It was one of only two times that we got put together in the same foster home. Man, I was happy about that. I remember that big old house—all messy—and I loved it. Mrs. Johnson was a lousy housekeeper. Man, she had four kids of her own besides us and another boy."

149

David was gesturing with a pizza slice in his hand. "But could she cook!" he remarked. "Remember those sweet potato pies? They were good people, Paul. I remember havin' this crazy hope. I kept thinkin' they'd adopt us or something, and we could stay there. Maybe they just didn't know how to adopt someone. But I sure wanted to stay there."

"Remember their big yard?" Paul recollected. "Overgrown weeds and rabbits. You really liked those rabbits."

"Yeah, the bunnies were cute," David replied. "The Johnson's house was up against a canyon. There was a lotta wildlife—skunks, raccoons, opossum . . ."

"You know, I remember one thing," Paul remarked. "When the coyotes showed up, no more bunnies."

"Yeah," David said sadly.

"You kept looking for the bunnies even when you knew what happened," Paul went on. "And you cried. I was so embarrassed. My thirteen-year-old brother was cryin' for the bunnies the coyotes got. I thought, 'What is wrong with this dude?' I didn't get it at all. But now I guess I do."

Paul looked directly at his brother. "You have a better heart than me, David. That's why you went to so much trouble to get that kid home. I didn't know Mom well, but I know she had a tender heart. I remember that. She was always gentle and kind, even when she was stoned. I must take after our father, the old *diablo* who stranded us all. But you take after Mom."

"Your heart's plenty good, Paul," David assured him.

"By the way, dude," Paul changed the subject. "I dropped Carmen off at her father's office. When she didn't come right down, I went up there. Hey, I saw a real hot chick, a blonde. She work there all the time?"

"Yeah, Livy Majors," David replied. "She's really nice. She helped me get Bobby Padilla home."

"Do you like her?" Paul asked.

"Sure, she's easy to work with," David said.

"No—I mean," Paul began.

"Man, don't even go there," David objected with a shudder. "She's a fine girl. She comes from a nice family. I wouldn't dare even think—"

"Dude, you're a good man," Paul said. "You made a mistake. You paid dearly for it. But you have a good heart and good character. You're good enough for any chick, and she'd be lucky to get you. If you like her, ask her out."

"No way," David objected. "It gives me nightmares to think of her ever finding out about me."

"Dude," Paul declared, "there's only one difference between you and a lot of other guys. You got caught, and they didn't. You learned from your mistake, and you paid the price. If you don't stop talking like that, man, I'll knock you upside your head." Paul dug into the box for another slice of pizza.

On Saturday morning, David was gassing up his truck at a station on Polk. Out of nowhere, a female voice shrieked, "Davy! Davy Morales!"

David turned to see Denise Valencia, his girlfriend before he went to prison. Old memories rushed into his mind. He had been in love with Denise, or at least he thought he'd been. She was his first serious relationship. She was pretty and fun, and she absolutely adored nice things. Among the many reasons David had for turning into a burglar was his desire to buy expensive gifts for Denise.

David looked at the girl. She hadn't changed much. She was still cute in her too-tight jeans and low-cut blouse. "Hi, Denise," he said.

"Oh, Davy! When did you get out?" she asked. "Somebody told me you were out. I didn't believe them 'cause I thought you'd get in touch with me first thing. But I didn't hear from you, so I thought you were still in the lockup. So how long you been out?"

153

"About a week or so," David answered.

"Bummer!" Denise groaned. "And you didn't call me, Davy. Hey, but you look great. Lotta guys getting out of prison look awful, but you're as handsome as ever. Boy oh boy, Davy, is it ever good to see you. I thought you'd be in prison for another couple years. I thought maybe we'd never see you again."

"I did everything right, and I got early parole," David explained. "You look good too, Denise. How've you been doing?" He pulled the hose from the gas pump and closed the cap. He wasn't sure how he felt about seeing Denise again. His feelings were very mixed.

"I'm a manicurist now," Denise answered. "I'm doing okay, I guess. Boy, Davy, didn't we have some good times, though? I thought of you a lot after you were gone."

David remembered going on dates with Denise. Augie and Freddy would bring their chicks too. The six of them would usually go to hot night spots, drinking, partying. "I've thought of those days too," David replied.

A look of sadness crossed Denise's face. "Davy, I felt so bad when you got busted. It wasn't fair that you took the fall like that. It just wasn't fair."

"I wouldn't rat out Augie, Denise," David stated. "He didn't force me to get mixed up in that stuff. I was old enough to know better. I wanted nice stuff, and I didn't make much money at that fried chicken house. I got greedy, and I paid for it. It was fair enough."

"Still, it wasn't right that he got off and you . . .," Denise repeated herself, still looking sad. "I thought a lot about writing you or going to see you in prison, Davy. I really wanted to. A couple times I started to write, but . . . then I didn't. I bet you thought I abandoned you."

"We all do the best we can," David remarked.

"Davy," Denise told him, "I feel so bad you thought I abandoned you. Are you busy right now? Could we maybe go and get a frozen yogurt or something? And, you know . . . talk?"

"I gotta get home right now," David responded. "I brought my laptop home to do some work. Maybe some other time."

Denise took a pen and a slip of paper from her purse. She jotted something on the paper and handed it to David. "Here's my cell phone number, Davy. Just call me anytime, and we can, you know, catch up. We had such good times."

"Yeah," David answered, taking the paper. "Hey, nice seeing you, Denise." He climbed into the pickup and drove off. He turned once and waved to the girl, who stood there looking forlorn. She still looked hot. She'd always looked hot.

As he drove home, David wasn't sure what he was feeling. He and Denise had some great times together. There was no denying that. David felt that, for a while, he loved her, and he thought she loved him.

David remembered the Christmas before he got busted. He'd bought Denise a pair of diamond solitaire earrings. He could still hear her screaming with joy as she put them on. David had never seen anyone so happy. Just seeing her like that made him happy too. The earrings cost over a thousand dollars. Denise hugged and kissed David over and over. It was the best gift she ever got, she told him. She didn't ask David where he got the money for such an expensive gift. But she had to know it wasn't from working at the fried chicken place.

Sometimes those days seemed like only yesterday. Other times, they seemed as though they all happened a million years ago. And they happened to someone else, not David. He and Augie would hit electronics stores about three times a week. For a while, they were making a lot of money.

David bought Denise a lot of nice things—clothing, jewelry—but he bought stuff for himself too. He went to good clothing stores and picked up expensive leather jackets. He got pretty much everything he'd always wanted. He remembered his teenaged brother's reaction. Paul would stare at the stuff and demand to know where David got the money. David put Paul off by telling him he was winning almost every night at the casinos. The truth was David lost more money at the casinos than he ever made. That motivated him to burglarize even more stores.

David didn't feel bitter about buying Denise all those nice gifts. That wouldn't be fair, he thought. She didn't ask him to become a criminal. They were both young, a little past twenty. They both drank and partied and lived as though there would never be a reckoning. David just got carried away by the easy money and lifestyle.

Then one night, when he was home with Paul, they were watching a baseball game on TV.

"Cops!" Paul had gasped.

The police were through the door in a second, their blinding lights in the boys' faces. David would never forget the ashen horror on Paul's face. The cops were shouting over and over, "Warrant! Get your hands in the air!"

David didn't resist arrest. He had no weapons. He never owned a gun in his life. He was devastated when the police officers put Paul on the floor too while they checked for guns in the house.

"He didn't know what was going on," David told the police. "My brother's just a kid. He's clean! He's clean! He never knew what I was doing . . . I swear."

Even now, David could feel his arms being jerked behind his back and the cuffing. It was the end of his life as a free man, the darkest moment of his life. He felt as if he were falling into a deep, dark pit and he would never get out. All of it was branded on David's brain: the terror and the shame of that night, the trial, the look on Paul's face as he sat in the courtroom and heard his brother sentenced to prison. No matter how long he lived, he would never forget that night.

But none of that was Denise's fault. He never blamed her. Not once. And now he looked at her cell phone number on the slip of paper. He folded it and put it into his wallet.

# CHAPTER NINE

Denise Valencia and David Morales never talked about his crimes. She knew David hung with Freddy and Augie, and they were always pulling capers. Denise just enjoyed the moment.

Denise came from a troubled background. She was a kid from a poor family. Her father had been busted for causing an accident while he was drunk. Someone was killed in the accident, and so her father was serving time. Her older brother was on drugs.

For that brief, almost fairy tale time, when she dated David, she had a good life. They traveled in style, ate at great restaurants, shopped at nice stores. It was like stepping into a bright new world that was exciting for both of them. Denise asked no questions.

When David was in prison, Denise never even sent him a card. He often wondered why. He thought about her a lot during that long, lonely time. He longed for any contact with the outside world. A small card on his birthday from Denise would have been wonderful. During the nights when he lay on his prison cot, he even fantasized that Denise might surprise him by showing up at visiting time. He thought that, when he got out of prison, they might get together again. He still cared for her then. But no letters, no card, no visits ever came. Denise told him she felt sad now because David thought she had abandoned him. But she had. And she never explained why.

None of David's friends wrote to him in prison. None came to see him. He didn't expect to see Freddy or Augie. Prisons spooked them. But he thought somebody from the fried chicken place might at least send him a card.

The only visitor David ever had was Paul. Paul also wrote letters and sent cards. Most importantly, Paul came to visit David every time they allowed visitors. He never missed. Paul was usually angry, especially in the beginning. He cussed David out. He berated him. He called him names. But he came. As time went by, Paul grew less angry. He started to talk about the future, when David would get out of prison. The brothers began to make plans, and thin shafts of light penetrated the total darkness of David's life.

David also joined the prison Bible study class run by Ivan Redondo, and that lifted his spirits too. For the hour and a half of the class, David felt like a normal human being again, not a convicted felon.

Those two things—Paul's faithfulness and the Bible class—saved David. But it was mostly Paul. He couldn't have made it without Paul. For those two years, he was adrift in a dark, dangerous ocean, and Paul was the rope he clung to. Before he went to prison, David had used some drugs. In prison, they were readily available, and everybody knew it. Without Paul, David would have gotten into drugs again and would have sunk forever beneath the dark sea.

The following Monday, David was working on Mr. Ibarra's business on his computer. Paul and Carmen came into his cubicle. Carmen came over and planted a kiss on David's cheek. "Whatcha doin', David?" she asked.

"Organizing some of the suggestions your father got at the meeting on the city budget," David answered. "The one cent sales tax increase won't go far, but it should help. We've got a bunch of bad options to consider for raising more money. Like the one about charging people fees when they make false fire and police calls. Some lady called nine-one-one to complain that gophers were eating her ice plant."

164

"That's a good idea," Carmen remarked. "Fine people for misusing nine-one-one. How dare people bother the firefighters and police for nonsense. They should chase the gophers on their own. I mean, how stupid can they be? If my cat gets stranded in the pepper tree, I'll go up on a ladder and get her down myself. The cat usually comes down on her own anyway."

"And then we can get more volunteers at the libraries and the parks," David said. "That'll save on paid staff salaries."

"I'll volunteer," Carmen said eagerly. "I love the library, but I like all the people who work there too. I don't want them to lose their jobs either, so that's a tough one."

"She's on a roll," Paul laughed.

"When I was gassing up my truck, I ran into Denise Valencia," David mentioned.

"I hope you told her to drop dead," Paul told him, his voice bitter.

"Whoa!" Carmen exclaimed. "Who's she?"

"Some creepy chick who used to hang with David. A gold digger. A barracuda in a bikini. Chicks like that give babes a bad name," Paul raved.

"That bad?" Carmen gasped.

"Worse," Paul responded. "If it wasn't against my principles to hit chicks, I'd send her into the next county."

"It wasn't her fault what happened to me," David stated flatly. "It was my own fault. I gave her expensive stuff, but she didn't demand it. I wanted to make her happy. I'm not shifting the blame onto her."

"You know what, dude?" Paul asked, throwing his arm around Carmen's shoulders. "I wanted to buy this chick here a cheap little gold chain with her birthstone gem in it. But she—"

"It wasn't cheap," Carmen cut in. "It was eighty dollars. Eighty dollars! No way are you gonna spend eighty dollars on some silly pendant for me. You work hard at the electronics store, and you need money for your filmmaking classes. I'm more than happy with a shiny pin from the drugstore."

"See?" Paul declared. "This is a treasure right here, man. She talks too much and eventually she's gonna drive me crazy, but she's worth it."

Paul grew serious. His arms were still around his girl when he spoke. "David, if that witch comes around our apartment looking for you, I'm gonna turn the hose on her. Fair warning."

Carmen poked Paul. "No!" she scolded.

During the next two weeks, two things happened to David that left him deeply confused. First, he was getting to like Livy Majors more every day. He found himself looking at her lovely profile and being very careful that she wouldn't catch him. Second, he frequently took Denise's cell phone number from his wallet and looked at it. He almost called her once. He was desperately lonely for a girl.

On a Wednesday at lunchtime, Livy asked David if he'd like to go down to the lobby coffee shop again. This time Jeff Caudillo wouldn't be with them. It would just be David and Livy. David was nervous. But the chance of being with Livy away from the office was so appealing that he accepted.

As they sat in the coffee shop, Livy asked, "Have you heard anything about Bobby Padilla since he got home? Is he back in school?"

"Yes, my friend Ernesto is keeping me posted," David answered. "Bobby's back in the freshman class, and he's doin' okay. Ernesto and the senior advisor teacher there at Chavez came up with a new program. They pair up seniors with freshmen kids who're at risk. The seniors kinda give the freshmen attention and help if they need it. Ernesto's buddy, Abel Ruiz, is paired with Bobby, and they're really hitting it off."

"Oh, that's wonderful, David," Livy responded, nibbling delicately at her scone.

Then she looked up and asked, "Do you like music?"

"Uh, yeah, I do," David said.

"There's going to be a really good jazz festival downtown in a couple days with some really great artists. I love jazz. How about you?" Livy asked.

"Yeah, I like it too," David replied. "Better than rock."

"Maybe we could go, then, if you're not busy with something else," Livy asked.

David turned numb. Was Livy asking him if he'd like to go somewhere with her? It sounded like that was what she was saying, but no way was that possible. David didn't know what to say. He couldn't say, "Sure, I'd love more than anything else in the world to go somewhere with you, Livy. But I'm an ex-convict, and you don't know that. So it wouldn't be fair for you to go thinking I'm a regular guy. If I told you about myself, you wouldn't want to go down to the corner for a taco with me."

Instead, David mumbled, "Yeah, that sounds nice."

"Oh, good, it's coming up this weekend, and we'll make plans," Livy said.

All afternoon, David thought about what he'd done, and he was miserable. This was wrong, he thought. He had to get out of it.

That night, Paul was on a date with Carmen. David dialed Denise's number. He knew he'd never have the relationship with Denise that they had before. But Denise knew about him and didn't care. And he just wanted to go to a movie and have something to eat with a girl. That's all he wanted.

"Oh, hi, Davy!" Denise bubbled when she heard his voice. She seemed genuinely happy to hear from him. To confirm that feeling, she said, "I was so hoping you'd call. I'd almost given up on you calling."

"Wanna go see a movie Friday night? Then we could get something to eat," David suggested. "That fish taco place."

"Oh, Davy! You remembered how I love fish tacos! I'd love to go," Denise gushed.

"Okay," David replied. "I'll pick you up around seven. You still livin' in the apartment on Oriole?"

"Same old, same old," Denise laughed. "Oh, Davy, I'm so glad you called. Oh, it's gonna be great fun to be with you again. I missed you, Davy. I really missed you. You're the greatest guy I ever knew."

When David picked Denise up on Friday night, she looked hot in a magenta sweater and skinny jeans. David glanced at her ears, where cheap hoops hung. He thought about the diamond earrings. What happened to them? Denise noticed him looking and explained.

"Oh, Davy, those diamond earrings were so fantastic. But I hit a bad patch, and I pawned them and then . . . you understand. Things are better now. I earn okay money in the salon. I do nails, mostly older women. You know, they don't look so good, but they want nice nails. It's really boring, but what else can I get? I dropped outta Chavez in my junior year, you know. I hated high school."

David wondered whether Denise had had any boyfriends since he went to prison. He couldn't imagine her sitting home on the weekends. "So, Denise, been seeing anybody I know?" he asked.

"You remember Antonio?" she answered. "We've gone out a few times." Antonio was a big hulky guy who drank too much and worked as a mechanic when he was sober. "I ain't seen him in a while. He's got a drinkin' problem. I went out with a coupla other guys, but, Davy, you spoiled it for other guys. You were always so special and nice. When you got arrested, I thought how unfair it was. You're a good guy. You didn't deserve to get locked up."

"No, Denise, I did the crimes," David insisted. "I stole from a lot of stores. I got a lotta money. I deserved what happened to me."

"You got a job now, David?" Denise asked. "Somebody told me you worked down at the city council. I couldn't believe it."

"Yeah, I have a good job," David replied. "I'm very grateful."

"Do you make a lot of money?" Denise asked.

"More than at the fried chicken place," David told her.

"Are the people nice down there? I've heard that all politicians are crooks," Denise remarked. "They get all they can from the people, and they don't deliver the goods."

"I work for Councilman Ibarra," David responded, a little annoyed. "He's a good, honest man. He's doin' a lot of good, and I'm proud to be able to help him."

They saw an action-adventure movie with a lot of special effects. David enjoyed the movie more than Denise did. For part of the time during the movie, she was texting her friends.

When David and Denise were last dating, they had often stopped at a little Mexican seafood place for fish tacos. They went there after the movie. It was still in business, and the tacos were as good as David remembered. Something about the sauce was spectacular.

"Wow!" Denise exclaimed. "Does this bring back memories!" After a few moments, she looked at David and asked, "Was it really awful in prison, Davy?"

"Not a good place to be," David answered.

"Did you get beat up and stuff?" Denise asked. "I've heard terrible stories about what happens to guys in prison." She dabbed taco sauce off her full, red lips.

"I stayed outta trouble," David said. "There are rules. Not only the prison authority rules, but the inmates' rules too. They're just as important. You don't crowd anybody. You don't hog the facilities. You try to respect the other inmates. I didn't have any serious trouble, but it was an experience I never want to repeat. I'm never going to do anything that'd get me in trouble again. I've learned my lesson."

"You know what's so great, Davy?" Denise commented. "You aren't changed. I thought you might come out of prison hard and bitter. It thought you'd be like a different person, but you're the same sweet guy I remember. I'm just so glad we got together again. I don't think a day went by that I didn't think about you and remember the good times we had."

David studied the girl. She was as beautiful as he had remembered her. She was even more beautiful than in his dreams, as he lay in that prison cell and longed for her. At one time in his life, he thought he would marry her and love her forever.

"Davy," Denise remarked, "you look so deep in thought. Are you thinking about the old days? Weren't they great? I had more fun with you than with anybody I ever knew. Only trouble was your brother. He

175

was such a little punk. He hated me. I think he always hated me."

David drank his soda slowly. He said nothing.

"Know what, Davy?" the girl went on. "I think your problem has always been your brother. He's been a real drag on you. I remember when we used to go out. He'd be there glaring at me, like I was evil or something. He really had a bad attitude. You guys are like night and day. I don't know how you stand living with him now. It must be awful."

David continued drinking his soda.

"He wore those hoodies and hung out with creepy guys," she rattled on. "He shoulda been the one going to prison, not you. You were always nice, but he can be so ugly. I bet he's done plenty of crimes that nobody knows about. His kind never gets caught. The cops are so stupid. They just nab poor guys like you while bad dudes like Paul get away."

David looked at Denise again, at her pale, smoky brown eyes and her long lashes.

176

She was wearing a lot of eye makeup, more than she used to. David tried to recall the days when he loved Denise. He tried to get in touch with the guy he used to be. But that guy seemed a stranger now.

Finally David spoke quietly. "When I was in prison, only one person stuck by me. I was so depressed that I thought I'd die of loneliness. I felt totally abandoned, except for this one person who gave me a lifeline. That was Paul, my brother. He saved me. He saved my life."

Denise seemed taken aback. "I wanted to come and see you, David," she began to prattle. "I swear I did. But I never been inside a prison before. It looked so cold and scary. I didn't even ever visit my father when he was in prison. I couldn't imagine goin' in there and being frisked and maybe the iron gates closin' behind me. I was even scared right after you were busted. I was worried that they'd come and arrest me for havin' the stolen diamond earrings."

"I didn't steal the diamond earrings. I paid for them," David told her.

"Yeah, I know that," Denise responded. "But I always thought maybe the money you used to buy them was from . . . you know, something illegal that you were doin'. I was so terrified that I'd get in trouble for havin' the earrings."

David finished his soda.

"I know it's wild, David," she went on. She was being defensive. "But I thought they'd somehow link me to whatever you guys were doin', you and Freddy and Augie. I think . . . I mean, I guess that's another reason I didn't come to see you in prison. I didn't want them to think I was, you know . . . part of . . . like a crime gang or something."

"So you knew I was burglarizing stores at night, Denise," David asked in a flat voice. "You knew that's where I was gettin' all the money for our good times and the gifts. You knew that me and the other guys were criminals. You figured that the diamond earrings weren't bought with money from the fried chicken place, right?"

"I never knew for sure," Denise admitted. "But, you know . . . I thought there was something going on. I tried not to think about it."

David took a long deep breath.

"Davy, you're out of prison now," Denise told him. "And all the bad things are behind you. You're home where you belong. Life can be good again for you—*for us*. Denise stared at David, who was not responding. "It'd be like old times, Davy."

David got up and went to the cash register to pay for the fish tacos and sodas.

Denise stood beside him. She tried to smile at him. Her perfect white teeth showed through her lips, wearing a shade of ruby lipstick that David always liked.

They went out to the pickup truck. Neither of them said much as they drove to Oriole Street.

In front of her apartment, David got out of the truck and walked Denise to the door. She drew close to him, as if she expected him to kiss her goodnight or, better yet, to come inside. But David said flatly, "'Night, Denise." He turned and walked back to his truck.

On the way home, David wondered why he even went out on a date with Denise. She was part of the reason he went to prison. He doubted whether she ever cared where the money came from. She just liked getting nice things. "Her and Augie and Freddy," David thought, "they all let me take the rap. They didn't really care whether that'd break me."

He stopped the truck at a curbside trash container. He tore up the little slip of paper with her phone number and let the small pieces flutter into the trash.

David could hear his brother's voice in his head: "Unbroken."

# CHAPTER TEN

That night, David Morales lay in bed, tossing and turning and unable to sleep. He thought about his prison record and how he'd screwed up his life. Maybe, he figured, he didn't deserve any better than Denise Valencia. Maybe he deserved no girl who was better and more decent and more compassionate than she was. But, David thought, if that's so, then he didn't want any girlfriend at all. He was sure of very little, but of that he was sure. There were worse things than loneliness, David believed, and being with Denise Valencia was one of those worse things.

At the other side of the room divider, Paul Morales spoke sleepily. "Dude, it's one in the morning. Why aren't you sleepin'?"

"How do you know I'm not sleeping?" David asked.

"You're thrashing around like a fish in a net, man. What's up with you?" Paul asked.

"Livy Majors," David explained, "the girl down in Mr. Ibarra's office. She thinks we're goin' to the jazz festival together on Sunday. I don't know how to get out of it."

"I thought you liked jazz, man," Paul said.

"You *know* what I'm saying," David groaned. "It's not fair to hang out with her when she doesn't know the truth about me. It's not right. She's a nice girl and—"

"Why don't you take her to lunch tomorrow?" Paul suggested. "You work there tomorrow, right? Just tell her the truth, and see what happens. It'll be fine, man."

"I can't, man," David groaned. "I can't frame the words. It's too ugly. I can't stand to see the look of shock on her face,"

"Would you *like* to go out with her, David?" Paul asked.

"Yeah, sure. Who wouldn't? She's really nice and I like her a lot," David responded.

"Okay," Paul ordered. "Take her to lunch. The right words'll come to you, man. It's a confession, bro. Even if she ices you out, you'll feel better. Now get some sleep." Paul turned over on his side and went to sleep.

"Yeah," David thought. "A confession. That'll take a load off my shoulders." He fell asleep shortly afterward.

On Saturday morning, David was at the office early. Because of the budget crisis in the city, Mr. Ibarra had asked his staff to come in for an unusual Saturday working day.

David had rehearsed how he would ask Livy to join him for lunch. He'd find a way to gently break the news to her that he wasn't who she thought he was.

David resolved that he wouldn't sugar-coat the truth. He'd admit that he burglarized a lot of stores at night. He'd tell her he probably would have continued if he hadn't been caught on a surveillance tape at one of the stores, leading the police to his apartment. David would admit to Livy that he didn't steal because he was hungry or lacked shelter. He stole out of greed. He just couldn't afford the good stuff that he and his high-maintenance chick wanted. His salary as a counterman at the fried chicken house just didn't cut it. He wouldn't blame Augie Rojas, although Augie did teach him the ropes and get him started on his short career of crime. He could have told Augie to take a hike, but he didn't.

Just thinking about telling Livy all this made David break out in a cold sweat, but he planned to do it anyway. He'd begun to like her a lot. If he had even a remote chance that she would accept him in spite of his past, he wanted that chance.

Jeff Caudillo came in, followed by Mr. Ibarra. The phones started ringing right away. A TV talk show host the night before had sounded the alarm about the "dark plans" of the city council.

David answered a few calls. Livy Majors came in. "I guess I'm late. I'm just not used to coming in on Saturday," she explained.

"No," Jeff responded, "you're not late. David and I are early. The talk show dudes are stirring up the mob, and we've got to be ready for the calls."

David glanced at Livy. She was wearing a pale green pullover and a dark skirt. She turned her head as if she felt his gaze and smiled.

"David, they just added a new jazz sensation to tomorrow's program. They said he sounds like Art Blakey. You know, that jazz icon who played with Blue Mitchell a long time ago. My father introduced me to his music. I have *Out of the Blue*. This guy Blakey was like a mentor to young kids coming up in jazz. The guy playing Sunday—Mike Corral—he's one of Blakey's discoveries."

"Sounds great," David responded, although he didn't recognize the people she was talking about. He wasn't into jazz as much as she was. David liked guys like Eric Clapton.

"You're coming, right?" Livy asked.

"Uh, yeah," David replied. His mind was spinning. Maybe he thought he *should* sugarcoat his past a little. Maybe he should say he just got into a little trouble and had to spend a few months in jail.

Two more phone calls came in.

"The condition of the Washington Street Park is an abomination," a man yelled. "Have you been in those restrooms lately?"

"No, sir, but—" David started to say.

"Well, stop sitting in your nice office collecting your huge salary," the irate man went on. "You tell Mr. Ibarra to bring his children to the restrooms at the Washington Street Park and see the filth for himself. I have two little ones who needed a restroom.

I'm telling you, it's a menace to health! You're gonna cut budgets, and you can't even supply decent services now!"

"Thank you, sir, for telling us," David told the man. "I'll get right on park maintenance and see that the condition is remedied. I agree with you that our citizens who use the park have a right to sanitary restrooms."

"There's no excuse to explain this indifference to public welfare," the man raved on. Then he said, "Whaddya say?"

"I said I agree with you, sir," David repeated. "We're gonna to take care of it. Thank you for giving us a heads-up."

"Well," the man said in a more peaceful voice, "I think it's our duty to speak up when we see something wrong."

"Yes, sir," David agreed.

When he put down the phone, he noticed it was a half hour to lunch. His knees got weak. Maybe, David thought, he should tell Livy about his bad childhood. He didn't like to talk about that, though. He thought it was a cop-out. A lot of kids came up through the foster care program, and they didn't end up as burglars.

Sure, some of David's foster parents were pretty bad, but most were okay. Usually, they were adequate and just indifferent. They weren't his parents. He couldn't expect them to act as if they were. Anyway, maybe if David had grown up in a nice home with loving parents, he would have done the same things. He met some guys in prison who had come from good homes and committed worse crimes than he did. Telling Livy about his miserable childhood would just make him sound like a whiney wimp.

David took a deep breath. Maybe, he thought, he should just skip the lunch *and* the jazz festival and crawl back under a rock.

During a lull, Livy said, "It's very informal at the jazz festival. We just pack lunches and sit on the grass. It's a lovely way to listen to music. I'm packing a nice lunch for us, David. I'm not a great cook, but I think you'll like it."

Before David knew it, he was riding down in the elevator with Livy. They were going to the coffee shop for lunch. Ordinarily, spending a lunch hour with Livy would have delighted him. He was liking her more every day. But thinking about his big confession gave him heartburn.

Even as they entered the shop, he didn't know exactly what to say. How could he tell her? "I don't know quite how to tell you this, Livy, but I'm a criminal—no, an ex-criminal. I'm on parole . . .." The words tasted like acid in his mouth.

"I always like plenty of mayo on my BLT," Livy remarked as they sat at the table. "It's not supposed to be good for you, but my Grandma loves it. She's eighty-five and going strong."

"That's wonderful," David responded, wondering if even lots of mayo would get his BLT down his dry throat. He began imagining her responses to his horror story.

He imagined how the conversation would go. "Oh no! How dreadful!" she would say. "I've never met an ex-convict before!"

"Yes, yes," he would say in response to her distress. "I'm so sorry I didn't tell you before. I was terrified of how you would react. Besides being a burglar, I'm also a coward."

"Were you in cells with murderers and all sorts of monsters?" she would ask.

"Well, actually I *had* a murderer in my cell at one time, but he was one of my better cell mates."

Livy smiled at David. She was trying to get a conversation going. "This is a really good sandwich, isn't it? I love it when they put on cucumber slices. The lettuce doesn't add much, but the cucumber is so nice and crunchy. You know, I'm packing liverwurst sandwiches for us tomorrow. When I was a little girl, my grandma always packed those when we went on picnics. And she put plenty of gherkins on the sandwiches. Just thinking about the gherkins makes my mouth water."

"Yes," David murmured, "I like gherkins too."

"You know what they are, don't you?" Livy asked, grinning.

"Uh, no," David admitted.

Livy giggled. "They're sweet little pickles. You'll love them on the liverwurst sandwiches," she explained.

David worked his way through the BLT, somehow getting it down by gulping soda. He thought he would tell Livy the ugly truth at the very end of their meal. Maybe the best time would be as they were walking toward the elevator. Yes, he thought, that would be best. He'd just blurt it out.

"Livy," he planned to say, "I should have told you this before. I'm an ex-convict who's been in prison for two years. I know you don't want to go to the jazz festival with someone like that."

Then, David thought, he would flee from the elevator and run to his desk on the upper floor.

But just then, as they were finishing lunch, a heavyset man appeared at David's elbow. "Are you one of Emilio Ibarra's henchmen?" he asked in a belligerent voice. He smelled strongly of liquor.

David tried to smile at the man in a friendly way. "What can I do for you, sir?" he asked.

Livy looked very nervous.

"You tell that blowhard somethin' for me," he growled. "We ain't givin' him and the other crooks in City Hall that pay raise they been wantin'. Not while they close down the fire stations and pull cops off the street."

"Sir, Mr. Ibarra is opposed to the pay raise for the council members," David responded. He stood up and put his own body between Livy and the angry man.

"You're friggin' lying," the red face man snarled. "I just heard it on the radio—Winky

Potts. Thank God we got a guy who tells it like it is. A man of the people. He said Ibarra's leadin' the fight to raise the council people's salaries. And he wants to take it out of the hides of the firefighters and cops. That's what Winky Potts said."

"Well, sir," David answered, moving even more between the angry man and Livy. "I believe you that Winky Potts said that, but it isn't true. Mr. Ibarra is dead set against any pay raises for the city council. He went further than that. He said he would refuse to accept a pay raise. You're right. A pay raise for the city council would be an outrage given the budget crisis."

The big man stared at David. "You ain't foolin' me, are ya?" he slurred the question. "Winky Potts's the best man on the radio, and I never knew him to lie. I listen to him religiously. I'd like to see Winky Potts governor of this state or president of the United States."

"Sounds good," David responded. "Thanks for giving me a chance to clear things up, sir. I'll watch for Winky Potts on the ballot."

The big man winked, gave David a thumbs-up, and lumbered away, very unsteadily. The manager of the coffee shop came over to David and Livy.

"Sorry about that," she apologized. "He's in here all the time. And loaded all the time. He hasn't ever caused trouble, so I can't do much about him.

"He's in no condition to drive," David remarked.

"No, you're right," the manager agreed. "But he's not driving. Lost his license about a year ago. Too many DUIs." The manager left them.

In the meantime, Livy Majors was doubled over laughing. "Oh my gosh, David, you were magnificent!" she told him. "I've never seen anything like it! *Where do you get that*?"

David shrugged. "Do you know Winky Potts? He's a liar and a jerk," he remarked. "He lies just to work people up so his ratings shoot up. He doesn't know the meaning of truth. Besides, could you really vote for someone called Winky Potts?"

Livy got up, and they walked toward the elevator. "I've heard him a few times," Livy replied. "He screams at the top of his lungs like a madman. Oh, David, come on. We'll be late getting back to the office! Let's grab that elevator and go."

They ran to the elevator just making it in before the doors closed.

Lunch was over, and David hadn't told Livy.

On Sunday, at eleven o'clock, David Morales drove to a nice suburban neighborhood near the community college. That was where Livy Majors lived with her family. They had a two-story stucco house with a Spanish tile roof. The lovely royal palms out front looked much prettier than the gangly Washington palms on the bird streets. The area was light years away from the *barrio*, away from Bluebird, Nuthatch, and those streets. Livy may have a Hispanic mother, but this was far from the *barrio*. Around here, you didn't find graffiti or boys in hoodies and baggy trousers. No homies hung around here.

David Morales kept asking himself what he was doing. He felt dishonest and selfish. He liked Livy Majors. When he looked at her, he felt warm and happy. But he had no right to her. Wanting her was wrong and stupid. It was rotten and unfair. He was taking her to the jazz festival under false pretenses. She thought he was a nice young man with a fine background. But he was a dirty rotten ex-burglar without the decency to come clean.

David entered the lovely house to meet Livy's good, honorable, wonderful parents. And doing that was as bad as telling a lie. When she did eventually find out about him—as surely she would—she would hate him for what he'd done. And she'd have the right to do so.

"David, this is my father, Andrew Majors," she said. "This is my mom, Socorro. Mom and Dad, this is David Morales, the young man I've been telling you about. He's transformed Councilman Ibarra's office. Before him, it was a fairly successful operation. Now it's a magical place where amazing things happen. We all just love him so much."

David shook hands with the parents. "Pleased to meet you," he said. "I'm really looking forward to seeing the concert with Livy."

He felt sick to his stomach, but he continued to be polite. "Livy helped me so much when we found this lost boy in the *barrio*," he told them. "I don't deserve all the credit for that. We worked together."

David managed to smile and nod and somehow get past talking for the rest of his short conversation with the parents. Then he led Livy to his pickup.

David drove toward the downtown festival.

On the way, Livy remarked, "This guy, Mike Corral. I'm just so excited to hear him. I'm in love with the guitar. Sadly, I'm no good at it at all. I've had lessons. But I think musical talent is something you either have or don't have."

"Yeah, I can't play anything either," David responded. He hoped she wouldn't ask him whether his fine parents had given him lessons on the piano or violin. It occurred to David that Livy didn't ask him any questions about his parents or his childhood. He thought she might be curious, but she never asked.

They parked and found a grassy spot near the festival stage. The musicians were set up, making last-minute tune-ups on their instruments. The big drums were already there.

"Look, David," Livy noted in a hushed voice. "There's Mike Corral. That guy in the blue shirt. I've seen him on TV. He looks like a nerd with those thick glasses, but he plays like an angel! Oh, wow! I'm so excited. I'm so glad we came."

David thought that right now, being here with Livy, he should be the happiest guy in the world. He should feel so lucky, so blessed. But his lie burned in his soul like a fire, destroying everything. Now it was too late to say anything.

Livy opened the basket and showed him the liverwurst sandwiches. "We'll eat at the intermission. Okay?" she suggested. "But it looks good, doesn't it? And it smells good!"

"Yeah, sure does," David agreed.

Livy suddenly looked right at David and spoke. "I know a girl shouldn't tell a guy she likes him until he tells her. But I'm sort of a weird girl. Ever since you came into Mr. Ibarra's office, I've been attracted to you so much. You just have something about you that's so endearing. But I don't know how you feel about me."

"I think you're beautiful and wonderful. I more than like you, Livy," David responded with a burst of emotion. He felt tears blurring his vision.

David was so desperately sorry. He hadn't played fair with this girl. He hadn't told her the truth right at the beginning. Now was a terrible time to tell her, but he had to. "Livy . . . there's a problem."

Livy Majors touched her finger to David's lips. "The other night," she told him softly, "I found out about you. Your brother, Paul, and his girlfriend, Carmen, invited me to that little place in your neighborhood, Hortencia's. They told me everything."

David stared at the girl. "*Everything?*" he gasped.

Livy smiled and reached over and grasped David's big hand with her small, delicate hand. "Everything. The parents you guys had, the foster homes, the burglaries, the two years in prison, everything. *Everything.*"

"And do you . . . ," David stammered. "Surely . . . I mean . . ."

She silenced him with a kiss on his lips.

Livy was holding his hand, and her gaze was on the stage. The emcee was warming up the crowd and getting ready to announce the act. The crowd was cheering and applauding.

But, to David, all that was a distant background sound. His thoughts were somewhere else. He had survived the foster care system in LA county. He had survived prison life. He had walked away from his old friends, who weren't friends at all.

Now, he had a career, not just a job. He had a wonderful girlfriend, not a gold digger. He had new friends-—real friends.

He looked down at Livy's hand, holding his. He had all this because, through all the hard times, he'd stayed . . .

"*Unbroken!*" Paul's voice resounded in his head.